PROLOGUE
SAUL

February

Saul clicked through his calendar while the conference call wrapped up. Interview with a potential project manager. Finance meeting. He didn't have a lunch break today, but that was probably for the best. He'd be too nervous to eat anyway.

After that was the big meeting.

He'd already told his executive team his news yesterday and they hadn't batted an eye. He didn't expect anyone else to either. He'd probably just say what he had to say, and then go on with the quarterly update.

But it felt huge to him.

He took a steadying breath and tried to focus on the meeting he was currently in.

"So we'll have the mock-ups to you by Tuesday. Any questions?" someone asked.

"No questions," Saul answered automatically.

He'd actually barely heard most of the call, but he wasn't worried. They'd already gone over the marketing plan and he'd worked with this advertising company in his old business. Switching from advertising a vanilla dating site to a kinky one shouldn't be a problem for them, especially since he knew one of the designers from a munch he used to attend.

People said their goodbyes and he hung up the phone.

He both wanted the whole-staff meeting to never arrive and wished it was over.

He looked at the clock in the corner of his screen. 10:58, so he had to get moving. At least interviewing someone would be a good distraction.

He picked up his tablet and flicked through his email to find the candidate's resume. Levi Cohen. The literal Jewiest name on the planet.

Well, presumably the guy wasn't too religious if he was applying to work at a kinky dating app.

In fact, it was much more likely that he was part of the BDSM community. Obviously, being a kinky little freak wasn't a job requirement for working at the fastest-growing kink-based relationship app on the market, but there weren't a lot of vanilla folks who worked at Cuffd either.

Even their building wasn't subtle. They shared an office with a few other companies, but the stylized logo out front didn't leave much to the imagination. An open handcuff formed the *c* and *u*, which attached to a

DEAR DADDY, PLEASE ME

REESE MORRISON

NAUGHTY OR NICE BOOK 4

Dear Daddy, Please Want Me (A Naughty or Nice Story)

Copyright © 2020 Reese Morrison

Cover Design: Cate Ashwood

length of chain for the entwined *f*'s, and looped around to connect with the closed cuff for the *d*.

It was Saul's baby. He'd happily sold off his old company, a successful mainstream dating app, for a pile of money and started up Cuffd in his free time. He liked start-ups much more than large corporations, and even though the customer base wasn't large, it felt like a service to the community.

Also, it was fun, and he felt like he got to be around his people.

Saul thumbed through the guy's credentials, which looked good. He was eminently qualified, had solid recommendations, and was ready to start work in about a month when his current company closed down their local branch.

Most importantly, Christy personally vouched for him. She was the project manager for the other development team and would be working with the new hire closely. She'd excused herself from the interview process, but they'd apparently gotten their computer science degrees together. If this Levi guy had been responsible and competent during group coding projects as an undergrad, he could only imagine that after a master's degree and a decade of experience, he'd be better.

Nikhil had already interviewed him over the phone, recommended him highly, and would be wrapping up his in-person interview right now. Honestly, even though Saul owned the company and would be working closely with whichever project manager they hired, it was

Nikhil's team. As the Chief Technical Officer, Saul trusted him to make the call. So if Saul didn't get any weird vibes from the guy, he would offer him the job today.

He just needed to focus for long enough to conduct the interview.

He snagged the tablet and straightened his jacket and tie automatically while he walked down the hall. It was only a few yards to the conference room where Nikhil and—What was his name? Oh, yeah, he smirked, Levi Cohen—were waiting for him.

And Levi did, indeed, look very Jewish when he spotted him through the glass wall. Lean and trim, with dark hair and dark eyes with the faintest wrinkles around them. He was smiling at whatever Nikhil was saying and, astonishingly, Nikhil was laughing. Nikhil was a great guy, but he could be a little up-tight. It wasn't often that he laughed out loud.

Saul slipped into the room and took a seat while the candidate, Levi, wrapped up whatever story he was telling.

"Hey," Nikhil greeted him. Then he turned back to Levi and they both stood to shake hands. "It was great talking with you again Levi. This is your last interview and you should be hearing from us soon."

"It was my pleasure," Levi replied. "Just remember, I'm calling Pickles Aren't Butt Plugs for my next band name."

Nikhil was still chuckling as he headed out the door. He paused only to give Saul a distinctive nod, which he interpreted to mean *hire him*. Good. That made things a lot easier.

Levi sat back down from the handshake and turned his attention to Saul. His eyes still sparkled with humor. He must have been at least a little nervous about being interviewed, but it didn't show in his warm demeanor. Saul didn't get the sense that he was overconfident or entitled, just that he genuinely liked people.

Saul wished he could be that outgoing. He tended to be on the quiet and intense side, though he loved his friends and family dearly and enjoyed running start-up companies. He just needed to psych himself up first and withdraw afterward.

"So, your next band name?" he started.

Levi shrugged, still grinning. "I don't actually play any instruments. Well, like violin when I was a kid. And, uh, that probably wasn't the best way to start out my interview, was it?"

He ducked his head like he was feeling bashful, but peeked up at Saul like he knew he was being cute.

It was a surprising look on a man dressed in a smart business suit and easily six feet tall.

Saul might have guessed he was a Dom, based on the way that he took up space, but that face was all naughty sub.

It completely transformed him. He went from rather average to adorable.

Kissable.

Not that Saul had any business thinking that about his new employee.

It did explain why Nikhil had liked him, though. The tall, muscular Chief Technical Officer was also submissive, and they'd probably bonded over that. Saul didn't know much of Nikhil's story, but he had the sense that he'd been hurt in the past and was a bit shy talking about it. So if Levi had drawn him out of his shell to joke around, that was another point in his favor.

Given where they worked, people didn't talk about their kinks as often as you might think, but it was usually something they shared pretty early. On the day-to-day, it was more like *you should ask so-and-so if you want feedback on how we present breath play,* and then you kind of went on with your work.

There were still a lot of unnecessary sex toys lying around the office, though.

Saul tried to get his mind focused again. He was all over the place today. "Actually, that was probably a great way to start the interview. There's obviously no requirement to be kinky to get a job here, but someone who stumbles over the word *butt plug* isn't going to be a good fit."

Levi raised his eyebrows, all pretend innocence. "Unless maybe the butt plug is really big?"

Saul rolled his eyes, but he was smiling.

He liked Levi's playful energy. He especially liked Levi's naughty boy look. Like he was hoping to get away with something, and maybe equally hoping that he'd get caught and punished. And now he was imagining what his potential new hire would look like walking around the office while trying to pretend he didn't have a toy in his ass.

So not what Saul needed to be thinking about.

"Alright," he turned the conversation around. "Why don't you tell me a little bit about yourself. What do you think of as your management style?"

Levi flew through the interview. He was confident without being brash, funny often at his own expense, and seemed to love his work. He was certainly competent, as Saul had expected, and had some great insights on the two sample scenarios that Saul gave him.

He was also a flirt.

Not in an aggressive way, though, more like he was sharing his enjoyment of the world and inviting anyone near him to bask in that glow.

Saul just happened to be lucky enough to be near him.

He just had this way of giving Saul all of his attention and making him feel like everything he said was special and important. He laughed at Saul's jokes, and his eyes lit up when Saul shared an idea.

It left Saul feeling relaxed and confident and… maybe crushing a little bit on the man who was probably going to be his employee in a few weeks.

He reminded himself that the zing he was feeling around Levi was probably what everyone felt. He reminded himself that Christy and Nikhil both thought he was the best candidate. He reminded himself that Levi had a decade of experience.

It wasn't like he was going to hire the man based on attraction alone.

Even if a job interview with Levi made him feel more alive and desired than any date or chat he'd had in years.

When his tablet chimed, he glanced at it automatically to see that the hour was almost up and he had to get to his next meeting.

He acknowledged the time, almost sorry to see it end. When he stood, Levi stood with him.

He reached out and shook his hand. "Well, Levi, let me be the first to say… Welcome to the team."

Levi's eyes blinked and then widened. "Really? I got the job?"

"Yep. Nikhil and I both agree that you're the best fit for the position and Christy recommends you highly. Nikhil will follow up with a formal offer, but if you want the job, it's yours."

Levi bobbed his shoulders in a cute little dance. It was another thing that might have looked silly on his large frame and formal attire, but instead he just looked happy and free.

Their hands were still clasped together. Maybe Levi had forgotten but Saul definitely hadn't. It felt like all his senses were focused on that warm stretch of skin.

"Thank you so much. Nikhil seems great, and I've heard good things about the team I'll be managing. And of course I'm looking forward to working with you, Sarah."

The two syllables crashed through him like ice water. Like the whole frozen surface of the lake had just split apart and dragged him down to its bitter depths.

He jerked his hand back, bracing against the table. He knew he needed to get a handle on it, but he needed a moment. He drew in a deep breath and let it out.

When he thought he could manage it, he looked at his newest employee. This wasn't at all how he wanted to have this conversation. He'd meant to have it at the beginning of the interview, during the introductions. Or better yet, to have Nikhil bring it up, though he'd only told him yesterday.

Alright, he could do this.

"I'm actually going by Saul now. He/him pronouns."

He held his breath, waiting for a response. Coming out as trans to his exec team had been nerve racking but fine. They'd all kind of nodded, like it was expected, and gone on with their days. Coming out to the whole company was going to be relegated to a PowerPoint slide, which was just how he wanted it. It wasn't supposed to be a big deal.

But for some reason, coming out to a new hire, especially one who he'd maybe imagined kissing a moment ago, seemed overwhelming. He hadn't prepared himself for this.

"Oh! Sorry about that," Levi responded easily. "I just assumed from your email, but that makes much more sense." He nodded his head like somehow it *did* make much more sense.

Saul let out a relieved sigh. "It's, um, new. I've been using the name for about a year with friends, but I'm announcing it to the rest of the office today."

That was what the big meeting was about. He only wanted to say it once, then preferably not discuss it again. It was just very... personal to talk about at work. He knew that almost everyone would take it in stride. If they didn't, his exec team would be more than capable of handling it, and Javier in HR would send around an email with some etiquette stuff for anyone who needed it.

But it had still kept him from sleeping for a week. In fact, the only time he'd really stopped talking about it was over the past hour when Levi distracted him.

"Well, congratulations, Saul!" Levi beamed. "I feel like I'm here for your birthday or something. Like, your first anniversary. No, that doesn't make sense. But next year you could call it your manniversary. Does anyone ever say that?"

"I have no idea."

"Well, then, let me be the first to congratulate you on your zeroth manniversary. I'm excited to be here for it."

"Uh, thanks." Saul wasn't quite sure how he felt but... much, much better than a moment ago.

"What's your middle name?"

And just like that, they were back to having a regular discussion.

"I actually haven't chosen one yet. My mother helped me decide on Saul. My father suggested that I take a name from my grandfather who passed last year but… his name was Eliyahu."

Levi cracked up. "Good Jewish name. You should keep it." He started to sing in a rich baritone and a dour expression. "Eliyahu hanavi, Eliyahu hatishbi!"

Saul only half-remembered the song from the end-of-Shabbat Havdalah services at Torah school. He knew it was about Elisha the prophet predicting the near arrival of a messiah who still hadn't turned up 3,000 years later, but that was about as far as he got. The tune was half dirge, half military triumph, a combination which he was certain only the Jews could pull off.

"You're one to talk, Levi Cohen."

"I know. My middle name is actually Moishe. No joke."

"Seriously? Yeah, so… Saul's enough for me in that department."

Levi cocked his head to the side. "I think the Latinate form of that name is Elias, if that helps. I always thought that was a sexy name. I mean, not that Eliyahu isn't sexy."

Saul laughed, but he was already turning the name around in his mind. He tested it out loud. "Saul Elias Kauffman. Yeah, I kind of like that." It didn't hurt that Levi thought it was sexy.

"Well, Saul Elias Kauffman"–Levi sought his hand

for a shake and this time Saul let him have it–"I look forward to working with you."

"Thank you. I do as well."

"And if you keep Elias, I want full credit for giving my new boss his sexy secret middle name during my job interview." Levi winked.

They were still holding hands. Where before the touch of skin had been a warm glow, now it sent sparks racing through him.

Levi hadn't exactly said that *Saul* was sexy. But even knowing that he thought his *name* was sexy, his new gender-affirming masculine name, was a huge ego boost right when he needed it.

He didn't want to let go of that strong hand, but of course he had to.

There would be absolutely no unprofessional behavior between them. No hopeless crushes. And nothing that could be considered favoritism.

But after Saul walked Levi back to Nikhil's desk, he managed to eat a bit of lunch while he walked through some of his ideas with the finance team.

And just before the all-staff meeting, he made a quick change to the slide.

Saul Elias Kauffman

(he/him)

Manniversary date: February 20

That should get him a laugh. He was starting to feel like everything would be OK.

1

___

LEVI

December

L evi drifted between awareness and slumber, settling into his favorite fantasy for falling asleep. He would be snuggled up on the couch with strong arms around him and Daddy's broad chest pressed to his back. Daddy would flick on a movie, snuggle him close, then reach down and start to trace over his cock through his thin pajama pants.

Daddy didn't have a specific face or identity, just a feeling of warmth and comfort. His hands were of no particular skin color as they traced over his bulge, but they were both sturdy and careful when he looked down to see them.

"Shhh…" Daddy would say when Levi arched up into his hand. "Watch the movie."

So Levi would lean back into Daddy's shoulder, while the din of a movie that had never been a real movie droned in the background. He would close his eyes and let Daddy take him away, with those endlessly teasing fingers.

Sometimes he'd get so aroused in this fantasy that he'd jerk himself until he couldn't stand it a minute longer and come all over his hands. Sometimes he just nestled in, one hand loosely holding his hard cock and the blankets curled up around him, until he drifted off. Either way, it was almost guaranteed to put him to sleep and lead to pleasant dreams.

Today was a floaty, dreamy day. Daddy was slow and gentle, almost hypnotizing. Levi's thoughts started to grow hazy and disconnected, Daddy slipping away to a warm sense of being safe and loved.

Loud music cut through Levi's dreams and he jerked awake. His heart was pounding, though his brain was still groggy. What was that sound? Why was it there?

His hand instinctively tightened on his cock and he moaned at the sensation. After just thinking about being edged like that, he could go off on a hair trigger. The only thing keeping him back was the annoying music.

The sound stopped abruptly and then started up again. He *knew* that sound. It was... Oh, right. His phone.

He reached under the throw pillow and dragged it out. He'd put it there for the alarm feature, but usually turned the sound off. The caller was listed as unknown, but the numbers seemed familiar. Not his own number, though, like a scammer. It was… Oh, right. The prefix for his job. This was work. Shit.

So… he should probably answer it. Ugh. This was going to ruin a perfectly good nap.

He thumbed across the green bar just as the jingle was reaching the end. "Hello?"

"Hey, Levi? It's Saul." Levi didn't need a name to know who it was. By the end of the first syllable, there were already warm shivers racing through him. He would know that mellow alto voice anywhere. "Uh, did I wake you?"

He settled back into the couch cushions and drew the fuzzy blanket back up. In his muddled state, the Daddy of his dreams acquired a face. Dark hair and dark eyes. Slim hands and rounded shoulders. A sweet little pudge of a belly that was hidden when he wore sharp, commanding suits, but which always drew Levi's eyes when he was lucky enough to glimpse him in a t-shirt.

Levi had been crushing on him since his job interview.

"Hey, Saul. I was sleepy, but I'm awake now." As soon as he said it, he realized it wasn't the right thing to say. He should have lied. Said he wasn't busy or something, and totally awake.

But it was Saul calling and he was still tangled up in dreams. If *Daddy* wanted to know what he was doing, he would tell him. When his *boss* called, he was supposed to be a professional. His mouth just hadn't gotten with the program.

"Lazy Shabbat nap?" Saul asked with a chuckle. Even his voice sounded like Daddy.

Levi nodded, then realized Saul couldn't see him. "It's a mitzvah to nap on Shabbat," he quipped. He liked to Jew it up around Saul, like their little inside joke.

"Really?" Saul sounded amused. "I think you're just supposed to refrain from work."

"Nope! It's actually in the Talmud. *Shayna b'Shabbat ta'anug.* Sleeping on Shabbat is a pleasure."

"Ha! I believe you. I barely made it through my ba–, er, bar mitzvah, but that sounds like something some rabbi would have said at some point. Then someone would have disagreed with him."

"Yeah, that was the point of the passage. You should take enjoyment on Shabbat, but the best enjoyment is Torah study. Something like that."

Levi found himself grinning. He was slowly waking up, but this relaxed back-and-forth with Saul was almost as good as dreaming. He could hear the smile in Saul's voice and imagine it in his eyes.

Levi's hand drifted down his belly. He wondered if Saul knew that it was a mitzvah to have sex on Shabbat, too.

He probably shouldn't mention that to his boss.

"Hey, um, why did you call?"

"I really hate to ask this, but we've got a pretty major bug somewhere and I can't track it down. Christy's sick and everyone else has already disappeared for Christmas."

"The whole development team?" He already knew

that Nikhil was in India for the whole month, but someone had to be around.

"Well, I haven't called anyone else yet. But since you're not celebrating Christmas…"

Levi groaned. He was going to spend the next hour repeating this same miserable can-you-come-in-to-work call with whoever on his and Christy's teams hadn't left town, and then working on it himself.

"…I thought maybe you'd be willing to come into the office and we could try to figure it out together."

Oh. That completely changed things. Levi's hand dipped a little farther. He had so many fantasies about being alone in that office together with Saul.

Completely inappropriate fantasies that it *might* not be the right time to indulge in.

"Um, sure! When do you want me?" He sure hoped that his voice didn't sound as husky and eager to Saul as it did to him. He had no game.

Also, he reminded himself for the seventy-zillionth time, he shouldn't be lusting after his boss.

"I'm already here so any time you can make it would be appreciated. Er, after dark that is."

After dark? There was a long pause while Levi's thoughts raced with suggestions. Alone in the office at night with Saul, the city lights laid out all around them while their voices echoed in the quiet rooms…

"I meant if you're *shomer Shabbos,* then I wouldn't ask you to work until Shabbat's over."

Oh. That wasn't nearly as exciting.

"I'm clearly not *shomer Shabbos.* I answered my

phone, right? I try to use it as a day off, though. Wander around the city, visit friends, that kind of thing." Strangely, they traded Jewish in-jokes all the time, but they'd never actually talked about their personal practices. He just knew that Saul was a lot less observant than he was.

"Do you have anything planned today? Or just prefer not to work?"

"Nope. I'm all yours." He needed to buy himself a muzzle. "I mean, I can be there in twenty, maybe thirty, minutes."

"Thank you, Levi. This means a lot to me."

Levi's heart definitely shouldn't have warmed with those words. He missed the next bit of whatever Saul said.

"...compensation at time and a half, you know, or convert it into vacation time."

Sure. Whatever. He knew all that. "Sounds good. I'll be there soon."

"Perfect. I'll text you so you have my number."

His number? Why would he need Saul's number? Not that he was complaining, of course.

"OK, bye!"

"Bye."

Levi's hand encircled his cock. Ugh. He could just imagine Saul's hand there, the way it would grip him tight. The way that Saul would stroke him to orgasm and then hold him while he slept.

Fuck. That line of thinking was totally not going to get him to work in twenty minutes. Why hadn't he said an hour? Maybe two hours, just to imagine Saul's hot gaze on him?

Totally inappropriate.

He crawled up off the couch, folded the blanket, and wrangled his protesting dick into his sexiest jeans.

If he was working on Shabbat, he could at least look good doing it.

You never knew who might be looking.

2

———

SAUL

Saul rested the desk phone in its cradle and picked up his cell, still going over their call in his head. Every word of it. Had that really happened?

Sleepy Levi was adorable, his voice thick and sweet like maple syrup. Even when he sounded more alert by the end of the call, he was still murmuring things under his breath that Saul was pretty sure he wasn't intended to hear.

Those little hums that escaped his lips were even better. He would bet that Levi had been touching himself. Or at least thinking dirty thoughts. He could have *sworn* he said something about sex on Shabbat being a mitzvah.

Which he *did* know, by the way. What twelve-year-old hadn't repeated that dirty fact to his friends?

With Levi, though, it sounded like he took it seriously. He was being goofy, something Saul found absolutely charming about him, but he could see sex with

Levi as something approaching a holy act. Taking delight in Shabbat, indeed.

It clearly hadn't been any sort of planned flirtation, which made it even sweeter. An intimate glimpse into everything that made Levi so appealing. His spontaneity and openness. His silliness and sincerity.

Add in those damn sexy whimpers and rapid little breaths, and Saul was already hard in his pants. He could just imagine Levi's slender chest rising and falling, the shape of his lips when his mouth opened.

Saul had been thinking about calling in a few more employees, but he couldn't quite bring himself to do it. He'd already clearly interrupted Levi in his sleepy-sexy dreams, and it felt like bringing anyone else into the office would be a further intrusion.

No, honestly, Saul just wanted Levi all to himself.

And that wasn't possible.

Saul sent a quick message to Levi with his phone number so he could let him into the building. He kept it short, just the basic info, then tucked the phone back into his pocket. No matter how tempting that gruffly sweet voice was, he was going to keep things strictly professional.

He had to. For a million reasons.

It wasn't the first time that he'd gone down this dangerous path in his mind. But after that dazzlingly erotic phone call—that conversation that never should have happened—he needed to remind himself why dragging the boy into his arms and kissing him until they were both breathless was a terrible idea.

OK, he could address this rationally. The first, of course, was that he was Levi's supervisor. Well, Levi didn't work for him directly. It wasn't like Saul did his evaluations. But as the CEO, Saul did set bonuses for everyone in the office. And if Nikhil ever left, there was a good chance that either Christy or Levi would be promoted into his position, and Saul would be the one making that choice. So Levi worked for him.

Even if, by some miracle, Levi were interested, the imbalance of power would make people doubt Saul's morals and Levi's abilities. They could both lose a lot of respect from their colleagues.

The more he thought about it, the more catastrophes he could imagine. Adding a D/s dynamic to a boss/employee relationship sounded sexy for a role play, but in reality it could be all too easy for him to take advantage without realizing that he was. Well, obviously, he'd keep the two strictly separate, and he got the sense that Levi was responsible and mature enough to do the same. But there was always the potential for it.

Which meant that he was off-limits.

Strictly off limits.

And if they *did* get together, what would ever happen if they broke up? It had disaster written all over it. He liked to think of his small company as something like friends and chosen family. They were all pretty relaxed with each other. As far as he could tell, most people liked coming to work and appreciated the opportunity to be themselves. So if there were a big office break-up and people started to take sides… Ugh. It had happened at his previous company and both employees had eventually quit, leaving chaos and frustration behind them. Of course, they'd been particularly immature about it and HR hadn't caught up with it until long after the damage was done. But still.

Looking back, people might even question the hiring decision. Because while nothing had happened between them in the year since Levi had joined the company, Saul couldn't deny the attraction that had raced through him every time he caught a glimpse of the man.

He'd assumed that it would go away in time. That Levi would be a perfectly competent employee, but lose his appeal once they got to know each other. Everyone had annoying habits and idiosyncrasies that got more frustrating over time. Or maybe the shine would simply wear off as Levi became an everyday fixture in the company.

Instead, the opposite had happened.

He just couldn't deny how his heart raced every time Levi strolled into his office with a report or a question. The way that his skin tingled when Levi smiled at something he'd said during a meeting. Some-times it was an eager smile. Sometimes Levi just looked… dreamy.

It was something that he'd learned to live with.

Also, if Saul was being strictly honest with himself, he wasn't sure if Levi was interested. He laughed and joked with everyone, which meant that Saul wasn't the only recipient of those flirty eyes.

There were some people who just sparkled, lighting up everyone around them. With someone like Levi, who was so completely in tune with whoever he was speaking with and genuinely excited about making a connection, he knew it would be all too easy to interpret it as something more.

Levi leveraged that skill as a project manager, too. He was competent and capable on the job, managing with a light hand while keeping everyone organized and motivated. His trust in his team showed in their efforts and high praise of his leadership.

Yet in hallway chatter or before meetings started, there was this silly side to him that poked up like a naughty boy. He'd say something funny and then look around with this little smile that said, *see how cute I am?* And Saul definitely did.

Sometimes he'd even turn that *I'm-so-cute* face on Saul and it looked like what he was really saying was *don't you want to take me home?*

Saul wanted to. Every time.

But if Saul were being honest with himself, the person who got that *I'm-so-cute* face the most was the other dev team project manager, Christy. And he knew there wasn't any attraction between them.

So he wouldn't be at all surprised if his burning crush was completely one-sided.

Add to that all of Saul's issues with his body and identity and there was no point in even considering it.

Saul had put off transitioning for so long, convincing himself that he wasn't sure or that he didn't need it. Now he was thirty-five, and going through puberty again, with all the zits and hormones and apparent self-absorption that it entailed.

Some days Saul was excited to shave the handful of hairs on his chin and see himself looking back in the mirror. With each month on testosterone, he could almost see his jaw becoming wider and his nose becoming slimmer. Going to the gym was like a dream because he could practically watch the muscles emerge from his previously flabby arms. And damn did he have a lot of energy to burn off.

There were some days, though, when he would see his reflection in a darkened store window and think, *who the fuck is that?* His hips were too wide, his chin was too round, and his ass was too big. People still said, "sir... I mean ma'am... I mean..." and ruined his fucking day.

Sometimes it felt like he was dressing up like a man instead of just being one.

And Levi? He was "gay all the way." Those were his exact words, thrown out casually in some forgotten conversation.

He probably liked men who looked like men.

Even ten months on T had shown Saul how *visual* attraction was for men. Before porn had been mildly interesting, mostly if it had novel kinks. Now Saul could catch sight of a muscular chest or a round ass and be instantly hard.

So he could understand someone not being attracted to his body. He didn't even want to be in it half the time. Maybe in another year or two or three, after the testosterone had time to work its magic and he'd made some decisions about which surgeries he'd wanted to get.

For right now, he wasn't sure he was ready for anything intimate. Sometimes just the idea of it made him freeze up.

If some hypothetical partner looked at him and laughed? Well, that was probably an exaggeration, though he heard that mocking laughter in his head sometimes. But even a respectful preference not to see or do anything with his body would slay him right now.

He already had enough of his own insecurities.

So it was really much safer not to think about anything that might potentially lead to taking off his clothes.

Especially not with a tall and lanky employee with luminous eyes and a naughty grin who could probably pick up any guy without a second thought.

None of those reasons stopped Saul from envisioning all sorts of dirty things, though. As long as those filthy fantasies stayed in his head, it couldn't hurt anyone, could it? He was determined not to actually do something, so he could allow himself to indulge for a moment. *Just* a moment.

When Levi had said "I'm all yours," it had sounded

like a promise. God, he could just imagine it. What would Levi be into?

Spankings? Bondage? A little edge of pain? A *lot* of pain? The list was potentially endless. He knew Levi was submissive, but since he wasn't into anything unusual enough to become the go-to person for feedback, and he didn't overshare like a few people Saul could name, that was all the info that he had.

Which was why this phone call was killing him.

What would Levi have done if he'd told him to take his hands off his cock? If he told him he'd been a bad boy for touching what wasn't his to touch?

Would he have whimpered? Moaned? Said, "yes, Sir"? Begged?

Knowing Levi, he would probably do all of them. Saul could just envision him submitting to every command in one breath and then begging for more in the next.

With a groan, Saul turned back to his computer. *He* was the one who needed to keep his hands where they belonged.

On the keyboard.

Debugging this stupid error.

LEVI

Levi had the whole freezing bike ride to work to realize how much of an idiot he'd been on the phone. The conversation was muddled in his head, but had he really been holding his dick while he talked to his boss?

Ugh. Super not cool.

He hoped that he hadn't given anything away.

Sure, he fantasized about Saul sometimes. OK, maybe a lot. But that was never supposed to cross the boundary into reality.

There was just this way that Saul looked at him sometimes. It usually came at the end of meetings, when the team had figured out what they were going to do and Saul gave them a summary. The words were always something about timelines and modules, but the look was pure Dom. Like he was giving commands and expecting them to be followed. Like he would be so *proud* when Levi did as he was told.

It made Levi shiver every time.

And God, how pathetic was that? Levi was almost forty and getting his kicks from meeting summaries.

He *wanted* to be dating.

No, what he wanted was a Daddy. Not in an age play sense. But he wanted someone to take care of him and dote on him. To punish him sometimes when he needed it. To hold him and keep him safe.

He was increasingly thinking that he just wasn't boy material, though. Half the Daddies took one look at him and weren't interested. The other half played with him a few times and *then* weren't interested.

There were a million reasons why. Too tall. Too plain. Too confident—yeah, that's what one guy had told him.

He'd been around the kink community enough to know that there wasn't any one body type for a boy— or a Daddy—but there were still trends. When he went to munches, the other subs tended to call him Sir until he set them straight. Everyone always accepted him as a sub as soon as he said it, but first impressions mattered.

When Levi walked into a room, people tended to pay attention. He stepped in and took control easily when it was necessary, smoothly filling in to facilitate when another leader wasn't appointed. He was self-assured at work and usually unflappable under strain. There was a reason he was a project manager, and he was damn good at his work, both the programming and people side of it.

Apparently when subs were confident, or at least when he was, it turned into being pushy. He didn't try to be pushy, though. In fact, he worked really hard *not* to be pushy.

The rest of the time he was kind of a goofball, which annoyed some Daddies, too. Apparently he couldn't be serious at the right times, though he felt like he used it more as a shield. His jocularity had been finely honed by years of being the shrimpy Jewish kid who was always picked last for kickball. Until he'd turned fifteen and was suddenly the too-tall Jewish kid who only had one friend to eat with at lunch.

When he'd realized that he was gay, it certainly didn't help his confidence any. He'd stared blankly when his friends talked about girls, then blushed at all the wrong times. College had been better, but he still thought of himself as that dweeby kid sometimes.

It was like his dating life and the rest of his existence were on two different planes.

Sometimes he couldn't even explain to himself why he wanted a Daddy. He had his life put together: a job he loved, good friends, a nice apartment in Goose Hollow, and a solid plan for the future. He didn't *need* a Daddy to take care of him.

But as soon as he got into a relationship, he'd find himself demanding all of his partner's time and energy and attention. Being needy. Greedy. Those were the worst accusations.

He'd thought that was supposed to be the point of

Daddy/boy relationships, but apparently there was cute-needy and annoying-needy. He was the latter one.

There it was. He wanted a Daddy who would spoil him, and it was looking more unlikely, or maybe impossible, with each passing year.

He zipped through the streets of the Pearl, Portland's downtown, grateful that the rain had let up for long enough to make it to the office. The damp pavement and small puddles would still leave specs on the bottom of his jeans, but it was unavoidable.

Ugh. Maybe he should consider vanilla dating. There were a few guys at shul who were cute, but… no, he really couldn't go down that path again. But where did that leave him?

He'd thought a few times about making a profile on Cuffd, but that just seemed too weird. There was no way that Christy wouldn't find it and tease him mercilessly. And using a competitor's app felt disloyal.

He forced his thoughts away from that sad line of reasoning and took note of the world around him. Sunlight gleamed off the streets and rainbows swirled in the oily residue. A surprisingly hardy cluster of pansies brought a burst of color to the small yard in front of one apartment building.

It was just a tiny patch of garden, but he was still envious of it. He loved the whole process of planting and weeding, watering and tending.

He'd love to have a house with a yard. Rooms full of sunlight and books and cozy furniture. And he could probably afford it. But the idea of it, having a whole house rattling around him by himself felt like admitting defeat.

That didn't mean that he couldn't imagine having his own garden. While he was dreaming, he might as well add a Daddy to take care of him and maybe a dog to greet him at the door.

But those were pipe dreams. Real estate was *way* too expensive, dogs needed space, and he'd learned that Daddies rarely took a second look at him.

Back to square one.

At least he loved his job. And if he enjoyed hanging out with his boss a little too much, well... a boy could always dream.

When Levi reached the front door of the office building, Saul was standing just behind the glass. He was looking at his phone, which gave Levi an extra moment to observe him.

Surprisingly, he was dressed down in a long-sleeve t-shirt that read "blood, sweat, and code" and a pair of dark jeans.

Except on a few days when they were doing sprints or special events and everyone in the company got a t-shirt, Saul dressed impeccably in well-cut suits and ties. That extra level of power and separation always fed into Levi's arousal.

Seeing Saul in a faded cotton shirt was intimate. It made Levi remember that they were going to be the only two people in the building. No matter how much he told himself to act professionally, he couldn't fight down the attraction. He wanted to touch.

He tapped on the glass and Saul looked up, startled. The moment he recognized Levi, his dark eyes crinkled and his full lips widened into a grin.

Was Levi wrong to think that smile was something special? It felt special.

Saul pressed the button to unlock the door, then darted back to greet him. "Hey, thanks so much for coming in. It means a lot to me." He reached out like he was going to push open the door, just as Levi gripped it himself and started to tug it open.

The wind was fighting with the door and Saul was blocking most of the frame, and he stepped the wrong way and stumbled against him. By the time he got inside, they were awkwardly tangled up together.

No, not awkwardly at all. Because Saul was somehow holding his wrist through his heavy rain jacket and had one arm wrapped around his back to guide him in.

Levi let himself be guided a couple steps into the warm lobby. He towered over Saul by at least six inches, but the position made him feel small and protected. If Saul slipped his hand down a little lower, it would be right at the small of his back. Was that on purpose or just some unconscious Dom thing? Levi wished he weren't wearing a coat so he could feel it more.

Levi had to remind himself to breathe.

"Sorry about that. I was just trying to get the door for you."

"I'll let you get it next time," he heard himself say.

He could feel his cheeks start to burn and hoped that it would just look like a reaction to the cold. That wasn't what he meant to say at all. Correcting it seemed like it would be even worse.

Saul quickly stepped away, pulling out his card to open the next set of double doors. The silence between them hung heavy. What had even happened?

In his dreams, Saul would push him up against the wall and kiss him, but in reality Levi had just embarrassed himself in front of his sexy boss. God, just because they worked at a kink company didn't mean that Saul thought of him as anything but an employee.

Fortunately, Saul either didn't notice or pretended not to. "I just gave you 24-hour access to our floor, but the building security is managed by another company so it won't go through till Monday. So if you need to leave and come back, just let me know so I can come down and fetch you."

Levi nodded. He liked the idea of Saul coming down to fetch him, though of course he didn't want to bother his CEO.

"Thank you," he said. That seemed appropriate. He needed to get out of his dirty fantasies and back to work.

They walked side-by-side across the lobby and Saul continued. "So I was thinking that maybe I could check the logs on the live site while you tried to replicate the error on a sandbox. I just finished replicating the current state of the site so you can mess around."

"That sounds good to me. What exactly is the error?"

Levi positioned himself off to the side as Saul pressed the button to call the elevator. Once they entered, he didn't even attempt to select their floor. He hadn't meant to say that stupid thing about the door, but now he felt like he was kind of bound to it. The elevator didn't even *have* a door that Saul could open, but he liked the idea of his Daddy opening doors for him.

Not that Saul was his Daddy or anything. He didn't even know what Saul was into. There was just something about him that was so…. Daddy.

The conversation that was happening in his head was very different from the one in the outside world. But that was always how it was when Saul was around.

"Basically, there seem to be couples who should have a very high compatibility rate, but they're not showing up in each others' match list. They can still search for each other by username, but the algorithm's gone wonky."

Huh. That was weird. "How do we know that?"

"We've had some users writing in about it. And you know that if five or six people bother to write in, there must be dozens of others who are just as annoyed and didn't bother to report it. The first one was a couple that was looking for a third, so the Dom was expecting to see his sub's account. We also have two pairs of friends who made profiles together and were just surprised. One set is in a pretty rural area, so it was an obvious miss when they were only getting two or three screens of matches total, when earlier they'd gotten twice that many."

Levi narrowed his eyes. "You know I don't know anything about the matching algorithm. It scares me." He shuddered for effect. He usually worked on interface design, cross-platform compatibility, and data storage. The matching stuff was Christy's baby and Saul poked around in it from time to time.

Saul grinned up at him. "It's not that bad. Anyway, we don't even know if it's a matching problem. I've been looking at it all day and I can't find a damned thing. There are a few more people who've emailed with complaints, but it's mostly an *I can't find this specific person on my match list even though they used to be there* thing. So the problem could be anywhere."

If Saul couldn't find it, that didn't bode well. Levi wrinkled his nose. "Better not be in the algorithm."

He thought he caught something in Saul's eyes just then. They landed on his scrunched up nose and then lingered on his lips. Like maybe Saul wanted to kiss him. Then it was gone, as quickly as it had appeared.

Levi tried to get his own face under control. He didn't know what it was that made him feel so silly and hopeful around Saul. Well, he did. But that didn't mean that Saul would think he was as cute as he liked to think he could be.

That was that too-tall, too-skinny, too-plain, too-pushy thing all over again. Being cute worked for cute people. He probably just sounded whiney.

Saul kept up the monologue as they walked down the hallways, going over potential issues he'd already checked and things he was considering.

Levi finally got his brain on track and asked what he hoped were good questions, but honestly, it seemed like the whole bug was a "who the fuck knows?" Because everything came back looking correct, except that a randomly selected third of the match results never showed up.

When Levi reached his cubicle, he sunk automatically into his chair while Saul perched on the edge of his desk.

That was all it took to get his mind completely off track again. Saul was so close, the outside of his thigh was practically brushing Levi's cheek. He could just lean forward a little bit and Daddy would guide his head down and…

"Thanks again so much for coming in today. I'll be in my office if you think of anything," Saul concluded.

And then he walked away. Dammit.

Levi had thought they were going to be working on this thing *together*. Like, maybe in Saul's office, sharing that elegant wooden desk. Or at least in a conference room or something.

Still, he couldn't help but lean back to watch Saul's ass until he disappeared around the corner. It was a luscious ass. A little curvier than other guys' and even tastier because of it. It was a delightful view, but apparently not for him.

Ugh.

Well, he was here anyway. He might as well do some work.

He flipped open his laptop which immediately turned on his other two monitors. That *was* the nice thing about being at his desk, he reminded himself.

He pulled open the sandbox, cleverly labeled with today's date, to start poking around. Now that he was here, he was actually curious.

The support ticket program turned up a handful of reports with the error, so he started there.

He opened a few incognito windows, which let him stay logged in to all of the different user accounts at the same time. First there was an existing couple looking for a third. The sub had written a cute letter describing how her Dom had told her she could invite someone else to play with them as a Christmas present.

Levi flicked between their two profiles. The sorting algorithm at Cuffd was supposed to take everything into account, including their checked interests like hard-core BDSM and an open relationship, as well as geography and sexual identity and preferences. He skimmed quickly down their kink lists and the two of them should have been a perfect match. When he searched for the Dom's name from the sub's account, indeed they were, with a 92% compatibility rating. But when he logged into the Dom's account, the sub wasn't showing up in his list at all. Weird.

He clicked on the next support ticket and looked up the profiles. He usually didn't notice much about what people entered, but this match was just too adorable. The profile picture of ArmyBratBoy showed two sweet young boys with tousled hair and dark eyes, looking exactly how Levi always thought boys should look. He found himself getting sucked into ArmyBratBoy's profile and messaging history.

Judging from his app history, ArmyBratBoy was a player. He'd contacted guys in several states, from the West Coast to the East over the past few months. Then, the night he'd written the letter to Santa, he'd changed his profile picture to the photo of him and the other boy and said he was looking for a Daddy with a heart big enough to love them both, so that they could stay together. Levi wondered what had changed in his life to switch from looking for "right now" to "relationship."

Because apparently they'd found someone. English-DaddyInNY certainly looked the part, stern and affectionate in equal measure. He said he was looking for a boy to spoil and care for, and apparently he was open to having two.

EnglishDaddyInNY had contacted the helpdesk after they'd met up, when ArmyBratBoy had apparently looked back at his profile to show the other boy, and it hadn't appeared in the match list.

Jealousy hit Levi something fierce. He never knew what happened to people after they met, but wanted it to work out for the trio.

More than that, he wanted it for himself. That dream of sending a few sentences out into cyberspace and having a Daddy come and swoop him up. Or at least that was how he imagined it.

He tried again with the other two pairs. There were two sets of friends who knew each other well enough that they'd expected to see each others' profiles in their lists. When he searched by their usernames, the other person came up with a high compatibility level. But that should have sent them to the top of the match results. Now that was really bizarre.

He couldn't see anything that was common across the profiles. One pair was in L.A. where it was easy to be flooded with compatible matches, but one pair was in rural Tennessee, where they'd set their geographic search range to a hundred miles. One sub had checked off nearly every kink, interest, identity, and compatibility on the list, and another was only into rope play with other gay men.

Ugh. This was going to take a long time. The matching algorithm was a behemoth, with hundreds of little quirks from so many people tinkering with it over time as they refined the weights that were placed on different components of the user profiles.

In addition, there was a learning algorithm that watched people's patterns of what they clicked on, who they wrote to, and who responded back. The learning algorithm spit out its own compatibility values that went into the larger algorithm, but what happened inside was a black box. The error could be on either side.

Or, of course, not in the algorithm at all.

So, first things first, Levi needed to replicate the problem. Still thinking of Saul leaning against his desk, he called the first profile PerfectDaddy. It wasn't like anyone else was going to see it anyway, and since he'd likely be spending most of the weekend at work he might as well amuse himself.

He filled it out fancifully, drawing on a mixture of knowledge about his boss and his own fantasies. Saul had brown hair and dark eyes, but there was nowhere on the form to mark the way that he made Levi feel all melty inside when his eyes crinkled up in a smile. He was short, maybe 5'7", though Levi gave him a generous 5'8". Though that didn't capture the way that he commanded the room during meetings, explaining requirements and giving motivational affirmations in a way that was unconsciously dominant.

During those meetings Levi hung on his every word to make sure he wasn't missing anything, but sometimes later he'd remember that tone of voice and imagine very different commands. And very different praise.

Then he started clicking interests. PerfectDaddy needed to be attracted to men, of course. He had to like spankings, because how else could he keep his boy in line? He needed to take their play out of the bedroom, at least some of the time, well maybe a lot of the time, when Levi was feeling needy and submissive. But he shouldn't be 24/7. Bondage, edging, role play, exhibitionism, sensory deprivation, chastity, definitely impact and pain play and... where was orgasm denial? He'd missed it and had to scroll back up.

Just checking all of them under PerfectDaddy's profile made Levi feel all shivery inside.

He skimmed back through the list and considered adding a few more. Maybe CBT? He loved watching it in porn, but he wasn't sure he was ready. Ooh... and sounding. He really wanted to try that. But it seemed like a lot to just click it, as if he knew what he was doing, so he left it off. The app didn't leave spaces for "soft limits" or "just curious." That was a constant back-and-forth conversation with the design team, but usually users found it too overwhelming.

There were a bunch of text boxes that he could fill out, but the matching algorithm just looked for keywords. He tossed in a couple for each box. *Daddy kink. Snuggles. Wandering around the city.* That one was a bit of an inside joke for the company because the algorithm liked to pick it up in people's profiles. He had no idea why.

He skipped to the next box. *Mexican food. Cooking. Talmud.* He snickered to himself at that one. Levi actually loved studying Torah, but he was mostly throwing that in there because of their conversation. It should also be rare enough to get him a quick match.

He knew now that Saul was more culturally than religiously Jewish, but that was fine with him. He'd dated non-Jews as well, so dating someone who was actually Jewish would be a nice bonus. Not that they were going to date or anything. This was just his fantasy played out as a tester account.

Next Levi started to make his own profile. Well, not his profile, of course. A generic sub's profile.

As soon as he clicked the "sub" designation, though, a window popped up with an obnoxious Santa head. Ah, right. That Dear Santa thing. He knew it was all over their advertising, but he'd kind of ignored it because a) Jewish, b) not his monkeys, and c) he wasn't quite desperate enough to use his own company's app and deal with Christy's teasing. He skimmed over the text.

Wishing for a Dominant of your own this Christmas?

Send a letter to Santa with a wish list describing your perfect match, and we'll share it with our Santa Doms and Dommes here at Cuffd. If one of them fits your list, they'll message you back with a simple question: Have you been naughty or nice this year?

It's up to you how you want to answer...

OK, it was kind of gimmicky and the overt Christmas theme made him cringe, but it was still a cute idea. Smirking, he called his profile JewBoy1. Then he started writing his letter.

Dear Santa,

It's hard to be a Jew on Christmas. Just like in that song that Cartman sings in South Park.

He paused to add a link to the video. If they kept this sandbox for a while, there was a good chance that

Christy would see it later, so he might as well amuse them both.

Nobody brings me presents, like sexy Daddies or candy cane mochas with whipped cream (because, let's be honest, that gingerbread shit is nasty, but I can totally be a sell-out to Christianity if it gets me candy canes in my caffeinated sugar).

So maybe you can work on that, Santa, for the Jewiest Jew Boy ever?

Love and kisses,

Levi

He sent the letter off into the cloud and then clicked through the profile. He made it the same as Perfect-Daddy's, including copy-pasting the text, except for identifying himself, er, the user, as a boy and sub.

Then he clicked between the two search results. There was PerfectDaddy, 98% compatible, less than 5 miles away, and online now.

If only real life could be like that.

He poked around with the output logs on the backend for a few minutes and everything looked fine. Then he checked PerfectDaddy's account for his Santa letter and there it was, right on top.

He changed a few settings with the location and distance, and still good. He started adding and removing kinks in JewBoy1, which lowered the compatibility quite a bit, but still kept the profile on the first screen or two of matches. Dammit.

He deleted the textbox with Talmud and his other interests, which dropped the compatibility lower than he expected. Well, maybe that was something to track down. He pasted the text back in and reset all of the kinks to the original matches, just for fun.

Alright, now he had one profile that was working. He needed to make another one that he could break.

He called this one JewBoy2. Because he might enjoy leaving jokes for Christy, but reliable names were still the best practice for test cases and he didn't want to have to remember what they were all called later. He started with his letter.

Dear Santa,

Do you know what I really want for Christmas? I want to know what's wrong with the matching algorithm.

Also, could Christmas be a little less Christmas-y? Like, how would you like it if all of the stores played Passover songs for a month every spring? Actually, making the country suffer through Dayenu and Ha Gad Ya on repeat would be hilarious. You should work on that, Santa.

Love and kisses,

Levi

P.S. Don't forget the sexy Daddy. I promise not to be too greedy. (Serious about that one.) Still waiting over here...

Nobody would ever see it, but at least he amused himself.

He filled in the rest of the profile, keeping the first few things the same, like the location and the top three or four kinks on the list, and then clicking more or less at random. He pasted the text from JewBoy1 into the first two boxes that were required but left the others blank.

He clicked on matches and…. Jackpot. Perfect-Daddy was nowhere to be found. He clicked back to the first account. Now, that was weird. The total *number* of hits was almost the same, 1,694 versus 1,711. He'd expected the number to decrease significantly.

He dug into the output logs, set them to display everything, and checked everything he could think of.

There was just *no reason* to have PerfectDaddy disappear. When he searched PerfectDaddy's name, there was a 77% match, more than good enough to make it onto the second or third page, which trailed off into the sixties.

He went back to PerfectDaddy's account and tried the reverse. JewBoy1 had an 84% compatibility and showed up just fine. JewBoy2 was missing. What the ever loving fuck?

OK, one more profile. He'd keep one matching, one broken, and one that he could mess around with.

JewBoy3. He was kind of looking forward to the Santa letter this time.

Dear Santa,

Happy Hanukkah! Just kidding. Hanukkah's over.

Now I'm just looking forward to the time-honored Jewish tradition of sitting on my couch, alone, eating Chinese food and watching movies on that random day in December when I have to take off work and no one wants to hang out. You know... Christmas.

So Santa, if you want to help a good little Jew boy out, how about a hot Daddy to watch cheesy movies with?

And since I've been so good this year, maybe make him a

nice Jewish man that I can bring home to my family on Passover? (Don't worry, I wouldn't tell them all the depraved things he does to me in bed.)

Love and kisses,

Levi

He clicked a few random boxes and checked the matches. No PerfectDaddy to be found and a 61% match.

Alright, maybe it was time to track it through the matching algorithm. I.e., his worst nightmare.

He started tracing through each of the features line by line, setting the program to spit out a step-through log for each module that he checked. He had to admit that the code was well-documented, but the whole thing was held together by bubblegum and duct tape. The legacy code never got thrown out and the modules had baby modules with little tiny yippy dog modules that should have just been put together in the first place.

It was kind of interesting reading them sometimes. Someone had put a *lot* of thought into matching switches up correctly, for example, since they might be interested in different things while acting as Doms than subs.

Someone had apparently put an equal amount of thought into putting categories of kinks together which served no real purpose that he could see. It was something like, if you liked shibari and general bondage and spankings you'd be in a different category than if you liked shibari and sensory play and edging, which could put you in a match category of people who liked some of those same things but also different ones... What the hell did that even mean? Wasn't the whole point of the checklist to just *check the things you wanted to do with someone else*? Why match someone to a person who didn't actually check the same things?

Well, the initials on whoever commented the code weren't ones he knew, so apparently they didn't work here any more.

He looked back and saw that the weight of the weird category module in the overall match was so low as to be almost irrelevant. Apparently this had turned out to be a stupid idea, which he could have told them in the first place.

This was why he didn't like the matching algorithm.

It did make him realize that he should probably look at the modules with more weight first. He dove into another module, but soon felt his eyes glazing over. Reading through large quantities of other people's code sucked. Reading output logs sucked. It wasn't the creative, energizing programming that he loved or even the satisfaction he got out of doing a more routine job efficiently.

Ugh.

He hated to do it, but maybe it was time to call Christy.

4

———

LEVI

Levi was about to hang up when Christy picked up the phone.

"Hello?" she whispered. "Levi?" She sounded wretched.

"Hey Christy, I think I should go. I was going to ask your advice on something, but it sounds like you're pretty sick. You should get some sleep."

"Hang on." There was a long pause and then she came back, speaking at a normal volume. "How's it going?"

"I'm fine. I mean, I'm working on the weekend, but how are *you?*"

"Much better now. I'm at my sister's house and we all got food poisoning last night. I'm pretty much over the worst of it. My sister's kids are sleeping it off in the living room, except the youngest one who thought shrimp were yucky. He's been climbing the walls since no one else is well enough to play with him. It's been quite the weekend. So here's my advice to the world: just say no to shrimp."

"Ugh. That sounds horrible, but I'm glad you're feeling better. And fortunately, I never eat shrimp anyway."

"Really? But they're so tasty!" As soon as she said it she groaned and they laughed together.

"I've seriously never tried one. They're treyf. Those ancient rabbis must have known there was something unclean about the little critters. I mean, they have so many skittery little legs! And, you know, food poisoning."

"You don't eat the legs. Now crab legs, those are tasty…"

"Treyf, treyf, treyf!" he spoke over her. He really did have a visceral reaction to food that he'd been taught his whole life was "dirty." When your religious rules said you couldn't even eat food that had touched it indirectly through an object that had been washed—you kind of developed an instinctive shudder.

"Alright," Christy snapped back to business. "What are you calling about?"

"Did Saul tell you anything earlier?"

"Nope. I was, like, on my fourteenth trip to the bathroom when he called this morning. Then I started retching and hung up. I'd say it was one of my finer moments."

"Oh, no. You didn't!" Levi would have been embarrassed forever.

"Yep. Honest truth. So what's going on?"

Levi explained the situation, dropping in some good-natured grousing about the superfluous modules. Christy had a few ideas, and even had him try one or two of them while she was on the phone.

Yeah, nothing.

"Dude, I don't know what to tell you," she finally said. "I mean, check out those other three modules I mentioned first, but if you and Saul haven't found it so far I can't think of anything in the matching algorithm. Do you want me to come in?"

"Nah. I mean, as much as I love your company, there's no reason to waste your time."

"Who else is there?"

"Just me and Saul."

"Ooh! How's that going?" she teased.

He rolled his eyes, even though she couldn't see him. "Christy, I have *no* idea what you're talking about."

He looked around, just to make extra sure that Saul wasn't nearby and that no one else had come in. He and Christy were always professional at work, but it hadn't taken her long to get him to spill his secret crush. After all, they'd been besties since college.

"Uh, huh. What's he doing right now? Is he making his stern Daddy face or his broody Daddy face? Or wait, the proud Daddy face?"

"Christy, I'm never talking to you again."

"No, wait. Did he bring you presents as a reward for working over the weekend? Did he make you eat all your dinner?"

"No! I'm in my office. He's in his office. I *thought* we

were going to work together, but I'm just sitting here in my cubicle, allllll alone. And lonely. Nothing is happening and your matching algorithm ought to die a terrible death."

"You ought to fix that."

"I can delete the matching algorithm right now."

"You know I didn't mean that. Go see what Daddy's doing. Maybe he needs a break."

"Ha, I wish. Anyway, it's not like you can talk." That was always his trick when she teased him about Saul. Change the topic.

"Oh, God. Tell me about it. Maybe I should quit my job. He'd be totally worth it, wouldn't he?"

"Nooooo! Don't leave me. Can't you two just have kinky, illicit office sex like normal people? I mean, we work for Cuffd, right? I'm sure Nikhil could get plenty of work done while he's kneeling at your feet in a jockstrap. You could set up a little work station for him under your desk and take out the ball gag for meetings."

"Ugh, I wish. You may have noticed that he's my direct supervisor. But Saul on the other hand…" she let it dangle.

They'd been over the conversation a million times. Her theory was that if Saul started dating Levi, that he might change some of the HR regulations. The two of them even had a whole drunken plan worked out where they gave each other performance reviews or something so their bosses didn't have to. Not that it would probably make anything better, since they were besties. Thank God they were both legitimately good at their jobs.

"Saul is far too responsible to date an employee. And I don't even know if he likes me."

He could almost hear her rolling her eyes through the phone.

"He likes you. He brings Kosher donuts to the office and then hovers by your desk until you follow him to the kitchen so you can pick the first one."

"Oh, yeah. And then he gives me the lovey Daddy face." He lived for that face. When Saul just seemed so happy to know that Levi was happy. Or maybe he was reading things into it.

"I knew I was forgetting something. Hang on, isn't there another one?"

"Yeah, the you're-being-naughty Daddy face. I have to work hard for that one."

"Levi, just go hang out with him. You know it's what you want to do anyway. Maybe there's some Hanukkah magic in the air. Like a Hallmark movie."

"Christy, do you know how many Hanukkah romance movies there are? Zero. No wait, there actually was one. It was… definitely a token effort by the movie industry to be multicultural or something. Anyway, Hanukkah's over. Hanukkah miracles? Done."

"Alright, porn's better anyway and this is the perfect set-up. All alone in the office with your boss, nobody around. And then you show up in his office in a jock-strap with some dance music and..."

"Hilarious. He'd probably flip out and make me put

my clothes back on. Then we'd never talk to each other again and I'd lose my job and have to move back in with my parents and be alone forever. The end."

"Just go hang out with him. You know he's too shy and proper to invite you in there. Maybe give him a little hint and see if he takes the bait. It's the perfect opportunity."

"Goodbye, Christy."

"Or wait. Just pretend that he's your Daddy. You don't have to act any different, just hang out with him, and live out your secret fantasy of debugging code in Daddy's office."

"You think that's what my secret fantasy is?"

"Um… I do, Levi. You just want to be near him so *Go. Do. It.* When he orders dinner on the company card, you can pretend it's your reward."

"I'm not that pathetic, Christy. I'll have you know that my secret fantasies involve a lot more programming getting done. I'd never fantasize about the matching algorithm."

"Ha! Bye, Levi. Good luck with the bug. Though maybe if you can't find it, you'll have to have a sleep-over in Daddy's office, so don't try too hard."

"Nope, definitely going home and sleeping after this. Alone. Merry Christmas."

"Happy Hanukkah."

"Hanukkah's over."

"What's the next one?"

"Purim. No, wait. Tu B'Shevat. It's the tree festival that no one cares about in, like, a month."

"Why is your tree festival in winter? OK, happy tuba-shuh-something, then. Go find Daddy!"

Levi hung up the phone in a better mood. If only it were as easy as that.

He clicked back to his JewBoy1 profile and put all of the settings back to his original interests. Perfect-Daddy was right there waiting for him.

Maybe he would make a real profile after this and look for a real Daddy. He wouldn't have to be perfect, just his.

And then he could stop mooning over his boss.

Because it would take a lot more than a Hanukkah miracle to get what he wanted.

He could go work in Saul's office though, probably. There was a conference table and a couch and everything. Honestly, if he didn't have this horrible crush, he probably would have suggested it anyway.

But would that just be teasing himself with something he couldn't have?

He made a deal with himself. He would test out the three modules Christy suggested, and then go find Saul.

He'd been a good boy and he deserved a treat.

5

SAUL

Saul rubbed his eyes. He'd been poking around at the app since this morning, combing through data. There just didn't seem to be a rhyme or reason to it.

Everyone was getting about two-thirds of the matches they were supposed to, but he couldn't find a single common factor to who showed up on whose profile and who didn't. All he knew was that more complaints had been coming in throughout the day.

He could only imagine how many people were missing connections right now, expecting to write back to someone they'd seen earlier who now appeared to be gone. He'd hate to have the media get ahold of this, especially while they had a big Christmas push going on.

The holiday didn't mean anything to him personally except for an odd week where everyone else took off work and he had some quiet days in the office. But the

Dear Santa advertising campaign they'd set up had brought in droves of new users hoping to find their match. Love it or hate it, it was difficult to avoid the pulse of Christmas, especially now that it was only a few days away.

He closed the window on the whole search chain he'd been working on, then stood to stretch his back. This really wasn't getting anywhere.

He thought about wandering out into the office to stretch his legs and maybe see how Levi was doing, but he didn't trust himself.

When Levi had looked up at him with those soulful eyes and said he'd let him get the door next time it sounded like… something more. An invitation to a tenuous dance of dominance and submission, spoken in a not-so-secret code.

He could be misinterpreting it, of course. But there was this pause where he almost thought Levi was expecting to be kissed.

He didn't know whether that was good or bad.

Of course, it was flattering as all hell to imagine that a hot guy might actually be interested in him. He'd obviously dated before transitioning, but although he'd always identified as pansexual, it was easier to date women. It let him be the butch one.

The world of gay men was a new planet that he wasn't quite sure would welcome him.

Then there was the fact that it was Levi. Levi with those playful eyes and flirty smiles. Levi who seemed to linger at the end of meetings just to walk down the hall with him.

That was why it was also a terrible thing. If Levi weren't his employee, he might at least work up his courage to ask him out.

But, he was. Better to stay in his office.

Saul sank back into his chair and opened a window to the sandbox. Maybe Levi had made some progress.

It took him only a moment to get a sense of what Levi had been up to. Lots of incremental error logs. A few usernames that he recognized from the support tickets.

He scrolled through a few more screens of report logs when something caught his eye. The words *Perfect-Daddy* seemed to jump from the page. The other account that was getting a lot of action was JewBoy3. They'd both been created today on a version of the platform that no one else had access to. Was there a JewBoy1 or JewBoy2?

Before he even opened the profiles, he started wondering. Was that Levi's kink? Did he want a Daddy? Those names couldn't be accidental, even if Levi was just messing around while he tested possible errors.

A shiver raced through him.

Saul had never thought of himself as a Daddy. When he'd been working so hard to force himself into a box that didn't fit, it hadn't seemed like an option. Being queer had been its own exploration. Then discovering kink. Recognizing and enacting his masculinity in the past year seemed like it was writing the rules all over again. And in between, he'd founded two successful companies, built them from the ground up, and sold them off to move on to the next thing.

So he'd thought a lot about being called Sir. But he hadn't explored any other identities.

He looked around, then tested the word out in the silence of his office. "Daddy."

OK, that sounded a bit weird. It wasn't like *he* wanted to call anyone Daddy.

But he could hear Levi saying it all too easily, in a hundred variations. Lightened by laughter as he joked around. Flirtatious and seductive when he knew just how sexy he was being. Frustrated and whiny with that little scrunch to his nose if Daddy wasn't giving him what he wanted.

But mostly Saul could imagine him, all sweet and serious, like he'd been at the doorway today. Saul was certain that Levi would like his Daddy to open doors for him. Not because he was weak or incapable, but because he wanted to be adored and taken care of.

Closely behind that thought was the breathless Levi on the phone earlier. He would pant Daddy's name, helpless and transfixed.

Saul knew he shouldn't open the tester profiles, but he did anyway.

The text was sparse, but he devoured it all. It was funny and quirky, just like Levi. As he compared the profiles and checked the logs, he became more certain that JewBoy1 had started out with Levi's actual kink list before he changed some of it for testing, because he'd changed it back to the same list. It was an exact match to PerfectDaddy's, which was the first profile he'd made.

It felt like Saul was getting a glimpse into Levi's secret world. Not that he hadn't read dozens of lists like this, shared on spreadsheets or on creased pieces of paper. Hell, Cuffd had a whole spin-off app just for this.

But if this really was Levi's list it was… special. Important.

He read through it again, imagining each act. He could give Levi all of that. Most of it he'd done before. A few things were lower on his list and some that he enjoyed weren't included. But overall, it was a very close match.

Vague longings for just being closer to Levi, maybe spending a bit more time together, started to coalesce into something tangible and lush.

He read over the text and the other details. Was this… was this supposed to be a message? The Talmud reference, funny as it was, had to refer to their earlier conversation. And everything else about PerfectDaddy, like his eye color and height, described him perfectly.

So what was that? Wishful thinking? An invitation?

Saul did the obvious thing and checked the match list for each profile. JewBoy1 showed up immediately. That was when he noticed the Dear Santa letter.

Snarky and witty, that was Levi. Saul slipped his headphones into his ears to listen to the song that Levi had linked. He wasn't sure how he'd missed it, since he watched South Park sometimes, but it was funny and irreverent, just the type of thing that Levi would enjoy.

Saul smiled to himself, thinking of Levi singing along and hamming it up. Even knowing what Levi liked in his coffee felt like a little gift.

When the song ended, Saul went back to read the letter and profile again, scouring them for clues. It was clear that Levi had filled them out quickly, and he even had the time stamps to check.

He flipped to JewBoy2's profile and read the second Dear Santa letter, which was just as funny, but not very helpful. Well, it cleared up one thing: Levi was definitely looking for a Daddy.

No, he read it again. There was something else there. What did Levi mean about being too greedy? And why was he serious about it when everything else seemed like a joke? Levi was one of the most generous people he knew. And if he meant "greedy" in a needy, sexy sense, that was good, right?

He logged in to the JewBoy3 profile, which at this point he was certain just held random selections because Levi was changing them all the time. The letter, though, felt like a personalized invitation.

Levi might still be joking about the holidays, but finding a "nice Jewish man" who would join his family on Passover *and* do depraved things to him in bed? That had to be Saul, right?

Or was he reading too much into it? Levi was

Jewish and all of his letters had been about Jewish stuff. This wasn't such a big stretch. It could be anyone.

He read through the few lines again. Just the idea of Levi thinking about him made his pulse beat faster.

It was on the third read that he found it. JewBoy1 had selected a height preference that went just below and above Saul's stature. It was probably stupid, but now he was certain that it was a message intended for him to find. Or if not that, it at least meant Levi was thinking about him. Right? Didn't it?

Levi was so slender and tall, but sometimes he almost ducked to make himself shorter. Saul, meanwhile, barely cleared five-seven. So for Levi to click that as a preference...

Saul's height was one of the things that bothered him most about his body. He'd missed the necessary hormonal surge in his teens, and no amount of T would fix that now. A lot of guys wouldn't date a man who was so much shorter than they were, but apparently, hopefully, Levi didn't care.

Saul clicked between the two profiles again. And again. There wasn't anything new there. It was just him and his morals and the sexy project manager who *worked for him* and might not be comfortable with Saul's frustrating body even though he'd practically put Saul's name on his tester account.

He wanted Levi to have his PerfectDaddy to watch movies with and eat Mexican food.

He wanted to *be* that Daddy.

Not that that changed anything about the situation.

He read the profiles again, though, torturing himself with possibilities.

Then he closed it. He needed to stop reading them. Maybe take a break.

He looked out the window to find the usual icy Portland rain coming down. But going outside might clear his head. He could certainly brave the miserable weather for a coffee.

Because Levi had only asked for one thing. Or at least only one thing that Saul could provide under the guise of a professional relationship. A candy cane mocha, which sounded more or less like a bucket of sugar with nostalgia sprinkled on top.

And he was damn well going to get that for his boy.

Well, not *his* boy.

His employee. Who was working overtime on a bug and deserved a thank you. Just like any other colleague. It was a perfectly reasonable thing to pick up.

And Levi would never have to know it was anything more. Right?

6

LEVI

When Levi checked the clock, his eyes were dry and his neck was hurting. Another hour gone and nothing to show for it.

Definitely time for a break. And a treat. He'd been here for four hours, and it wouldn't be at all inappropriate to knock on Saul's door to see what he was up to.

He stepped into the corridor to stretch, swinging his arms out to the sides and twisting at the waist.

Just as he was twisting back around, he spotted Saul at the very end of the corridor. And was he holding coffee cups?

He smirked, thinking about Christy's Hanukkah miracles. Maybe this was a sign?

He twisted in the other direction while he waited for Saul to come closer, but when he turned back around, Saul was just standing there.

Watching him.

Hmmmm… Levi twisted back the first way, just to see what would happen. He was pretty sure that Saul didn't realize he'd spotted him. After all, there were dozens of cubicles worth of space between them.

Broody Daddy's eyebrows were knit into V. What was he thinking?

The professional thing would be for Levi to say hello and talk about the bug.

But Christy had been giving him ideas. Plus, he'd checked all three modules, so he deserved a treat. And he *liked* having Saul's attention.

He stretched again, bending backward until his shirt rose up. He didn't have a lot of assets to flaunt, but he could always tease.

He stole a glance at Saul. He still hadn't moved, his gaze focused on that patch of skin, eyes stormy and intense.

It made Levi feel all shivery inside. Like his stringy physique and gangly limbs were actually sexy.

Saul had backed around the corner a bit, but he was still watching.

Levi wished he had more ideas for stretching, maybe some pole dancer moves. Yeah, no. But he could improvise.

He snagged his desk chair and wedged it against the wall, then put one foot on it and bent over to touch his toes. Or at least as close as he could reach. Totally legitimate stretch, right? Could he help it if his ass just happened to be in the air?

He shifted and twisted a little bit, hoping Saul was

enjoying the show. And that he wasn't making a complete fool of himself.

He stood up to check, keeping his head down and to the side.

Oh, that was exciting. He'd have to call this new expression *dirty Daddy face*, because Saul definitely liked what he saw.

He switched to the other side.

The stretch felt good. Having Saul's eyes on him felt even better.

He could hear footsteps coming down the hall now, so he took his time bending first one knee and then the other. His ass was kind of flat, but he moved it sinuously.

Stupid? Maybe. Fun? Definitely. He sometimes didn't think things through too well when Saul was around.

Saul had to feel the attraction too, right? Levi felt breathless just being around him.

When he sensed that Saul was just a couple feet away, he finally turned.

"Saul!" he squealed. OK, maybe he'd overdone that a little but, well, he was excited. He could hear Christy's suggestion still playing in his mind. If he *pretended* Saul was his Daddy for the day, he wouldn't actually have to know, right? "Did you bring me coffee?"

"Yeah, I um, got some coffee. If you want it. You've been working hard, so I think it would be a good rewa- thank you for coming in."

Uh, huh. That word had definitely been *reward*.

Maybe they were more on the same page than he thought.

If Christy could be trusted, well…. Maybe there wasn't a Hanukkah miracle waiting for him, but at least he could spend an evening pretending.

"Oh, I do want it! I think my brain is melting. I need treats to sustain me." Levi clapped his hands in delight.

Inner boy: 1, Professionalism: 0. God, he was an idiot around Saul.

"I think you need dinner to sustain you." That was stern Daddy.

Oh, hell yes. With that voice, if Daddy wanted him to eat dinner, he would lick his plate clean.

"I mean, um, it's on the company. When you work weekends."

Sure it was. Daddy was buying him dinner.

And was Saul blushing now? A shy Daddy was kind of adorable. He didn't think he'd ever seen Saul nervous before.

Had *he* made Saul nervous? It didn't seem possible. Nothing fazed Saul. They'd found an employee stealing money from the company and Saul had narrowed his eyebrows and bit out a few terse instructions. They'd been hit with some bad press when someone using their app made a bad choice, and his eyes had widened before he set up all the calls he had to make. And talking about kinks, like whether spanking should be categorized under impact play or get its own header, was daily business.

Yet Saul was definitely blushing.

He stepped in close, letting his excitement show. "What did you bring me?"

Saul shrugged, but his eyes said something different. "Peppermint? I know you like those sugary drinks, so I hoped this might be OK."

"Ooh! That's not peppermint. It's *candy cane.* You guessed my favorite! Yes, please." Levi made grabby hands.

Saul made the lovey Daddy face, smiling like giving Levi the drink had made his day.

Levi carefully cupped it to his chest, bent his head, and said, "Thank you, Saul," in his sweetest voice.

Saul's voice was rough and the pink in his cheeks deepened when he finally managed to grunt out a "you're welcome."

Out of all the crappy holiday drinks out there, Saul had picked the good one. He couldn't think of a clearer sign than that.

Daddy clearly knew what Levi needed. Daddy wanted to give it to him.

And the office was still empty except for the two of them.

What could he do to make Saul's eyes light up again?

The coffee was *definitely* still too hot to drink, but he pressed it to his lips, tilted it back, and closed his eyes in ecstasy. OK, so maybe that was a little over the top. But it smelled divine, and if he were really drinking it that's exactly what he would do.

He hummed his appreciation deep in his chest as he met Saul's eyes. Dark and striking, they looked like they wanted to devour him. Dirty Daddy.

Hell yeah.

He knew that he was playing with fire, but couldn't he have this one little thing? Just one evening pretending that he had a Daddy who wanted to take care of him? He felt pretty certain now that Saul would indulge him as long as he didn't cross any lines.

They'd been subtly flirting for months. Or maybe not-so-subtly, since Christy had picked up on it. But she knew him.

This could just be an extension of that. A little more flirting. A little more time together. It didn't have to be a Hallmark movie or a porn video, but if Levi could just soak up a little bit more of Saul's attention, he'd take every bit of it. There was no one here to see them after all.

The only problem, as he saw it, was that Saul was a good guy: scrupulous, responsible, head of the company. If he hit on Levi, it would probably be sexual harassment or something since he was in a position of power.

Of course, that position of power thing was a whole fantasy in itself, being called into Saul's office and bent over his desk... But that wasn't very helpful right now.

In reality, even if Saul was thinking the same dirty thoughts, he would probably be too moral to act on them.

So Levi would have to give Daddy a little nudge. Just a tiny one.

"I need a change of scenery," he declared. "And I'm bored. Wanna hang out in one of the conference rooms? Ooh! Or could I work in your office? That has the best view."

Saul's eyes widened, then the broody eyebrows were back. "Um, sure. I'll, uh, make sure the table's cleared off." Saul turned to go.

Nervous Daddy was cute. The table in his office was almost always clear, so that had just been an excuse to sneak away. Levi regularly had meetings there with the other managers, so all of this nervousness was just for him.

He didn't really want to make Saul nervous of course. Just push him over whatever was holding him back and spend some time together.

Levi watched appreciatively as Saul strode down the hallway. He walked with such strength of purpose, his legs eating up the ground despite his short stature. Sure, his hips were a bit wider than most men's, but then again, everybody had a different body shape. It was more the commanding way he held his body that always got Levi going.

Saul looked back as he turned the corner and Levi didn't even pretend he wasn't watching. He thought about blowing a kiss, but gave a fluttery-fingered wave instead.

Saul disappeared.

So… this was either going to be the best thing that

ever happened to him or he'd totally screwed everything up.

Hopefully Saul would want to hang out with him.

Hopefully he'd still have a job on Monday.

God, he was such an idiot around Saul.

7

———

SAUL

S aul ducked around the corner and then collapsed against the wall. He put one hand over his heart, as though the pressure could slow down the rapid beat.

OK, that was flirting. That was definitely flirting. Awkward, over-the-top flirting, yes, but all in Levi's signature style.

That was Levi looking so sweet and happy and pleased with his gift. Levi making sure he caught a glimpse of skin and blinking those wide eyes at him. Levi moaning like there was an orgasm captured in that cup and he'd just let it out.

Now what the hell was Saul supposed to do?

He retreated to his office and stood in front of the table where he often held meetings. There were a few papers scattered on it, but picking them up didn't quiet his racing thoughts.

Levi wanted a Daddy. Levi, inexplicably, seemed to want *him* as a Daddy.

Could he do that? All of his concerns from before hadn't changed. It still wasn't ethical. Levi might still have a lot of issues with Saul's body. Hell, *Saul* might have a lot of issues with his body.

But then there was the way that Levi had clapped his hands and practically bounced with delight when he saw that coffee. It should have looked incongruous on an almost forty-year-old man, but instead he just looked liberated, like he was free from the stresses of his everyday life and unafraid of how he might be perceived.

How could Saul want to do anything less than make him that happy all the time?

He was so fucked.

He glanced down at the papers he was clutching, wondering how long he'd been staring off into space. The writing on them didn't make any sense, inconsequential with everything else going on. They were… oh, yeah. Agendas and a project team financial report. Nothing he needed.

He tossed them in his recycling bin. Now what? Should he move his laptop to the table? Stay at his desk? Staying at his desk would probably send the message that he needed to send: that they were colleagues and nothing more. But if Levi were any other colleague, of course they would sit at the table together. Catch twenty-two.

He gathered up his laptop and moved it to the table. There. Perfectly normal.

The best thing he could figure out was just playing

it cool. Just because Levi was irrepressibly sexy, and apparently interested, didn't mean that he needed to act on it.

They'd sit at the same table and try to track down the error. They'd order some dinner at some point and eat it. Eventually, they'd either find the bug or give up for the evening. That was it.

Alright. He could do this.

Where was Levi though? He was sure that at least ten minutes had passed while he'd been woolgathering. Had Levi changed his mind? Realized what a terrible idea this was? Decided to avoid him?

Saul headed back into the hall. Even while he was walking, he told himself that chasing down an employee wasn't appropriate. But he just… wanted to catch a glimpse of him. He at least needed to know.

The distinctive whir and thud of a vending machine drew his attention before he could get too far. Saul peeked into the company kitchen where Levi was retrieving a package of cookies from the tray to go with the potato chips in his other hand.

"That's not a real meal," Saul heard himself saying.

Levi spun to look at him, eyes sparkling. "No?"

Oh, Levi was going to be a handful.

"I thought maybe I deserved a treat. But I suppose I have to eat dinner first?"

Dammit. It seemed like every word out of his mouth carried a double meaning. Like he was waiting for Saul to deny him the treats now and parcel them out later for being good. Like he wanted Saul to bring him his meals.

Saul tried to convince himself that he was just reading into things. That he was adding context that wasn't there now that he knew what Levi was into. It was a stretch.

Because Levi was watching him, hands behind his back in either a display of submission or because he was hiding the treats he'd tried to sneak. His expression was just begging for a kiss or a spanking.

It was fascinating how the line between naughty boy and willing sub crossed and wove around itself.

Saul had to admit that it was a rush. He didn't want to *really* control every aspect of a partner's life. But being trusted to take care of someone in small, visible ways? Yeah, he wanted that.

He forced himself not to respond. Not to stride across the kitchen and kiss those impish lips until they were both breathless. "I'll pull up some menus and meet you in the conference room."

Then he beat a hasty retreat.

He had his laptop set up and at least appeared to be working by the time Levi came in.

"Hey," he said without looking up. There was no way that he could concentrate, though, when he could still track Levi in his peripheral vision.

Levi, naturally, took the chair right next to him instead of any of the other four that were available. Saul had settled at the head of the table without thinking much about it beyond having elbow room, and now Levi was sitting just around the corner. He wouldn't be able to look up without seeing him.

Levi fiddled around with cables for a moment, then sat down.

Their legs brushed. No, more than brushed. Levi sunk down in his chair until one of his long legs was tucked under Saul's calves, heat flowing between them.

Saul kept his screen open, but Levi had all his attention.

The boy hummed and wriggled in his chair as he typed, like an excited puppy.

There was just something different about him today. Maybe it was just seeing him outside of normal business hours. Or maybe it had started with that sleepy, sexy phone call.

It wasn't just his flirtatious comments, but the way he moved. His limbs were relaxed, but he vibrated with a sinuous energy. He almost glowed. Like something had been set free inside him. Something a little playful, maybe a little bratty.

It was everything that always set off a spark when Saul was around Levi, but instead of getting it in little glimpses, he was getting the whole bonfire. And the gooey s'mores, too.

Being responsible right now was going to require a whole different level of determination. By orders of magnitude.

He could cut it off, of course. Address it directly, remind Levi that it wasn't appropriate, and probably never have Levi give him that hopeful, teasing look again.

He argued the other way. They weren't *actually* doing anything wrong. And Levi just seemed so… happy. So as long as Saul didn't encourage him, that was OK, right? Levi could be himself, Saul would make sure they stayed focused on their work, and everything would be fine.

Levi's stomach rumbled, and Saul suddenly felt bad about chastising him for the snacks.

"Ready to order dinner?" Saul still kept his eyes on the screen and reminded himself that he always ordered dinner for employees working on the weekend.

He opened a new window to pull up the menu for the one Kosher place that delivered to the office. Not that he'd looked that up before or anything.

"Sure. I eat veggie out, and otherwise I'm down for anything." Levi gave him a beaming smile.

Huh. He hadn't realized that. *Veggie out* was the Jewish code word for keeping Kosher at home, but eating restaurant food that wasn't certified Kosher as long as it was vegetarian. Everyone knew that it had touched utensils and surfaces that had touched meat, which technically wasn't supposed to happen, but it was kind of the thought that counted.

Levi's Jewish practice was much more complex than he'd thought. Then again, he hadn't expected him to work on Shabbat. Of course, Jewish practice wasn't just one thing. He knew a lot of people who kept

Kosher even as they dropped a lot of other traditions. And who was he to judge? He'd grown up eating bacon cheeseburgers.

Saul honestly didn't think much about his Jewish roots day to day, but with Levi around he found himself thinking about it more. Or maybe he just wanted to know everything about his tempting employee.

"So… Chinese? Mexican? Thai? There's a Kosher deli that might deliver, too."

"Mmmmm…. Those all sound good. Thank you."

Saul finally looked up to find Levi giving him a dreamy look. What was going through his head? He didn't seem to have any further thoughts on dinner. He'd just said *thank you*.

Then it really sank in. Levi was waiting for him to choose. Trusting him to take care of him. Giving him, perhaps, the opportunity to do this little thing as his Daddy. It was a heady feeling. And it wasn't *technically* crossing any lines.

"Great. I'll order something." Saul said, probably more brusquely than he intended. He already felt like he wasn't reading from the right script.

Levi was supposed to say, *Thank you for ordering for me, Daddy.*

And he would say, *I need to make sure that my boy is eating something healthy, but I got you a treat, too. Something much better than those vending machine cookies.*

That was how it worked, right? It was sure as hell what his mind was filling in right now.

He also felt like he had to get it right. Like if he didn't order the right thing, he'd be messing something up. It should have felt like a heavy responsibility but instead it felt like… an opportunity. A way to communicate to Levi something that he probably had no business communicating.

Thank God for the profiles.

He pulled up his favorite Mexican place and got what was definitely too much food. Vegetarian enchiladas. Cheese flautas. Chiles rellenos. A hearty salad with hard boiled eggs replacing the chicken. Three types of vegetarian tacos. Then tres leches cake for dessert. Whatever Levi's palate, there had to be something he would like.

He would be paying for this himself instead of expensing it, but Levi didn't need to know that.

He submitted the order, then tried to get back to the data. He really wasn't getting anywhere. Not that it was a huge surprise, but at least earlier today he'd been able to focus.

Now he just kept noticing Levi's leg resting against his.

He put together a few queries to pull a report that he was pretty certain he'd already pulled this morning.

Levi pressed their knees together.

Saul sorted a spreadsheet.

Levi said he wanted to tell him what he'd been working on and get his feedback, which seemed like a welcome distraction from, well, his distraction.

Levi started with an efficient summary, but that

only lasted until they were looking at two of the error profiles. Levi got all heart-eyed talking about how sweet it was that EnglishDaddyInNY had found Army-BratBoy and his friend.

Saul was almost jealous for a minute. He would never be as tall and rugged as the Daddy in that trio. The man looked like everything a Daddy was supposed to: dominant, distinguished, and well… just *male.* Very, very masculine, with his well-groomed beard and his muscular shoulders. He was young, maybe in his thirties, but he had piercing blue eyes that could only come from a place of great confidence.

If that was what Levi wanted, Saul would definitely be a disappointment.

But Levi didn't mention the Daddy's looks. His focus was all on how lucky the boys were that they had someone to take care of them. How they would get spankings *and* cuddles. How sweet it was that they found each other.

Levi didn't have the slightest bit of subtlety, which only made it cuter. His hints were about as subtle as a sledgehammer. Saul found himself smiling, getting drawn into Levi's fanciful story about three people he'd never know beyond their profiles and a perfunctory message to the help desk.

Saul probably shouldn't have found it so charming, but there was something earnest about Levi's excitement. Even if Saul hadn't stumbled over Levi's three letters earlier, there wasn't any doubt now about what he wanted.

Which raised another question. Why today? What was different from every other day in the past year or so that had brought on this adorably clumsy seduction? If it could be called such a thing.

It was more like Levi was hoping that if he acted enough like a boy, whatever that meant to him, he could somehow trick Saul into wanting to be his Daddy.

It was working.

When the demonstration was over, Saul thanked Levi for his summary and tried to ignore the flash of disappointment that crossed Levi's eyes. He didn't like that look at all.

If he were somewhere else... Hell, if he were *someone* else, he would snatch Levi up in an instant.

He focused pointedly on his screen. He pulled another report and barely even saw it. Time ticked by.

Levi interrupted the silence. "Hey, can I play some Hanukkah music?"

Saul squinted his eyes. "Hanukkah's over." And, God, Hanukkah music? The only song he could think of was *Maoz Tzur,* or *Rock of Ages,* which sounded like a dirge and had horrible lyrics about bloodthirsty killings and racial superiority once you read it in English. Maybe Adam Sandler's spoof? Oh, and the kiddy songs like *Dreidel, Dreidel, Dreidel.* He vaguely remembered one about latkes that had hand motions.

He wasn't listening to any music that had hand motions.

"I know." Levi rolled his eyes. "But they're so much fun!"

He was so going to regret this. "Sure."

Levi had clearly already pulled something up, because he tapped his mouse pad and music burst into the room. It was… not bad. Kind of fun, actually. A kicking beat, smooth voices and… "Hang on, is this Taylor Swift's 'Shake it Off'?"

"Yep!" Levi did a little dance move and sang along. "I'm feeling pretty great! Bum dum dee dum. Got latkes on my plate! Bum dum dee dum."

Saul felt a smile forming on his lips. He was never going to get anything done, but did it matter? It wasn't like he'd caught the bug in the past nine hours, and he was unlikely to find it now.

Being around Levi was both calming and energizing, and his joy was infectious. This wasn't some practiced seduction, but instead a more innocent revelation of Levi's personality.

He really *liked* Levi. And his goofy innocence somehow added to that thrill of desire.

The next song was a parody of Bohemian Rhapsody, with ridiculous lyrics. The "I'm just a poor boy, nobody loves me" bit had been replaced with "Kindle the lights, remember the Maccabees. How did those five boys lead us to victoryyyyyyy-eeeeee—eeeeee?" Levi closed his eyes and sang his heart out.

The cuteness was overwhelming.

Then they moved on to a compilation of Star Wars melodies with, yes, the words of "Rock of Ages" thrown in. And some random Hanukkah words. There was some sort of singing war between latkes, the potato pancakes, and sufganiyot, the fried jelly donuts. It was silly and irreverent, and yes, extremely singable.

Levi was laughing at something on the screen and he tilted it toward Saul. The singers were dressed in full-on Star Wars costumes, acting out movie scenes while they sang about latkes.

"Where do you even find this stuff?"

"Oh, the Maccabeats and Six13 have dozens of songs. There's a bunch of YouTube channels that have hours of this."

Huh. The Maccabeats name was obviously from Maccabees, the Jewish rebels who starred in the Hanukkah story. Saul had to dredge up his Torah school memories to figure out the other name. That was it. There were supposed to be 613 mitzvot, the bizarre collection of good deeds and practices to avoid.

It was a wonder that Levi's chair was still holding him in. He shimmied and danced and snapped through the playlist. His timing and pitch was sometimes a little off, but his sheer enthusiasm easily made up for it.

The next was a parody of "Dynamite." The chorus was undeniably catchy. "I flip my latkes in the air sometimes, singing aaaay-oh, spin the dreidel. Just wanna celebrate for all eight nights, singing aaaay-oh, light the candles."

Saul almost wanted to join in, but his voice had just started cracking. The rest of the time it was too high.

He didn't think that Levi would mind but, well, it wasn't how he wanted to present himself.

Were Daddies supposed to be serious? Or did they goof off with their boys? Saul was serious by nature, and in the past his kink-based relationships had only made him more so. Being around Levi was like an invitation to goof off.

Or maybe not quite that. An invitation to enjoy Levi's goofy enthusiasm, to give it a chance to expand and take root.

No, that wasn't what he was supposed to be thinking about.

By the time they got to a Hamilton parody, Saul could see that this wasn't going to end. "Can you work with that on?" he asked gently.

Levi looked up like he'd just been caught being naughty. Maybe on purpose. "I was taking a break?" he asked with false innocence.

Saul could feel himself getting sucked into this Daddy thing. It was apparently about a lot more than just kink. Or maybe it was just Levi's magic. "Was it a nice break?"

"Mmmm-hmmmm. I'm much more ready to focus now," he said innocently. Saul could easily envision him trying to wheedle his way out of a punishment.

Definitely a handful, that one.

Levi lowered the volume, but he continued to hum along and bop his head in time to the music.

Saul poked around randomly in the database. There wasn't a damn thing he hadn't tried already, and watching Levi was much more compelling anyway. He went over some of his outputs from earlier.

After about three more songs, Saul finally had a flash of inspiration. He set up a query, searched it, formatted the data, and… nothing.

He looked up in exasperation, only to find Levi gazing at him adoringly. The boy didn't even pretend that he wasn't watching him. He just gave a saucy wink and got back to work.

His flirting was so over the top that Saul felt his lips quirking up in a smile. There was sexy and suave, and then there was just… silly. Levi had crossed that line a while ago, and it was kind of adorable.

And yet *also* sexy. He just wanted to reach out and touch, to run his fingers through that hair and kiss those lips that were still moving silently in time with an upbeat version of "O Hanukkah."

His thoughts were interrupted when his phone buzzed. The food had arrived and he went downstairs to fetch it.

When he came back up, Levi had closed both laptops and dredged up two mismatched place settings from the kitchen and dimmed the lights.

Saul rolled his eyes when he saw it, because, seriously? But he was smiling at the same time.

Saul's defenses were crumbling fast. He wasn't quite sure what this was. A seduction? A game? A playful flirtation to pass the time? Either way, he was blown away that Levi had chosen to let himself go around him.

He could hardly remember his objections when he

laid out their meal from the two bulging bags. Levi oohed and ahhed over the selections, thanking him in that joyously sweet way.

He's your employee, he reminded himself. *You should just tell him that nothing can happen before this goes any further.*

He couldn't bring himself to do it, though. Not when Levi was scooping little bits of each dish onto his plate and humming in appreciation when he took his first bite.

Not when he shoved half a taco in his mouth to keep it from falling apart, then looked helplessly at Saul because his mouth was too full to talk.

Not when he somehow got a dab of whipped cream from the tres leches cake on his nose and Saul wiped it off with a napkin.

And not when he took his last bite, then leaned back in his chair in a show of satisfaction.

"That was delicious," he murmured sleepily. "Now I just need a cozy nap." He stretched and wiggled from his seat.

Oh, yes. The nap that Saul had interrupted earlier.

"You could take a nap on the couch," Saul offered. His office had a plain black, industrial-style couch that faced his desk. There were three sections covered with that easy-to-clean and hard-to-destroy plasticky fabric and metal arms. It wasn't the most comfortable, but he'd slept there before when he'd had crazy deadlines.

He already knew that he'd spend Levi's whole nap watching over him. He could even tuck him in with the throw blanket he kept in the bottom drawer of one of the cabinets.

Levi gave the couch a longing look, but then shook his head. "If I sleep this late in the evening, I'll never sleep tonight." He sighed theatrically. "I suppose we should get back to work. Once we find this thing we can go home."

The words stopped Saul cold. Whatever this thing was, it was about to end. It hadn't even started yet. Hadn't been anything.

But on Monday, they would both go back to work, and Levi would be his usual, responsible self with a twinkle in his eye. And Saul would go back to his drab existence.

He didn't quite know what was going on, but he was pretty certain that if he gave it up now, he wouldn't get another chance.

Was that what he wanted?

No, he knew what he wanted. Well, mostly.

But was that what was right?

He opened his laptop again, staring sightlessly at some random profile's match list. He'd looked at the same screen so often that he didn't really see it.

Someone had dressed the interface up a bit for their holiday promo, adding some sparkle to the top and a glittery sheen to the background colors that displayed the match percentages. It seemed appropriate for the sparkling feeling of the day.

Saul vaguely remembered approving that work, then hearing that it had been put off because of something else. Apparently the color scheme alterations had gone live and it looked pretty good. He'd have to compliment whoever had worked on it on Monday.

That was when he saw it. The bug.

The user had matches from 100% to 98%. Then from 95% to 93%. Then 90% to 88%. He scrolled to the next page and it continued. 70% to 68%. 65% to 63%.

He clicked on another profile at random and checked their matches. Nothing that ended in a 7, 6, 2, or 1. He tried another one.

Holy shit. Whatever color or shade was supposed to get those middle percentages wasn't there and the matches weren't there either.

"Hey, uh, Levi?" He should tell him. He should really tell him.

He was humming along to a Hanukkah parody of what sounded like Kanye while he typed. "Yeah?"

"Who did the new color scheme? With the glitter?"

"Oh, that was Jazz. We thought we wouldn't have time for it, she said she could get it done on Thursday before she left on vacation. It looks pretty good doesn't it?"

"Yeah," he agreed faintly.

It took him less than a minute to find the faulty module. The percent ranges in the comments didn't match the percentages in the actual code, so the programmer must have made a last-minute change.

He switched all of the ranges to end in 6's and 1's, then pushed out the module to the live site. Since the matches ran on the cloud, it didn't even need an update to the app.

When he reloaded the match list he had open, the hits went from 1,232 to 1,788. The full range of match percentages showed, in all of their glittery glory.

He tried one of the couples who'd written in, just to be sure. Yep. There it was.

That was it. They could go home.

It was a let-down, after all the time he'd put in searching for it.

No, that wasn't it. It felt like an ending.

He flipped back to the sandbox version where Levi was still working and clicked on PerfectDaddy. He read it all again.

The profile wasn't really filled out, but the checklist looked complete. He could do that. He could *be* that. Probably. Maybe.

He wasn't like BritishDaddy or whoever that guy was, a nameless set of data points on a screen. Levi knew him as a person. And somehow still seemed to want him.

He clicked on PerfectDaddy's matches, where JewBoy1 showed up right on top. He still couldn't see JewBoy2, since he hadn't made the changes in Levi's copy of the site. He clicked on JewBoy1's letter.

Levi wanted a sexy Daddy and a candy cane mocha with whipped cream. He signed it love and kisses, from the Jewiest Jew boy ever. He wanted a nice Jewish man to take home to his parents. He promised not to be too greedy. (Seriously.)

Levi was just so happy and silly and adorable, and for some reason he, apparently, wanted Saul to be his Daddy.

Could he really take that risk? There were a thousand things that could go wrong, starting with losing the respect of all of his employees and ending with Levi breaking his heart. Somewhere in the middle was the instinctive fear that Levi would find his body repulsive.

Levi threw his head back dramatically, singing "oooh-ooh-oooooh, the latke recipe…" to the tune of "Shut Up And Dance."

What would it be like having that innocent delight in his life every day? Saul was sure that Levi had difficult days. Everyone did, though he'd never gotten a glimpse of them at work. But he found that he wanted to be there for those too.

Not to mention all the dirty thoughts of the past year, which seemed to be exploding today. Levi with his ass red, eyes glassy with pleasure and his face streaked with tears. Levi bound helplessly and begging him to come. Levi blushing and thrilled when he made him perform in front of an audience.

Saul took a deep breath. He tried to consider whether he could balance his personal and work life if he were dating an employee, but that just led to other thoughts. Like having Levi sit at his feet while he worked. Calling him into the office to inspect his cock cage. If there were ever a company that wouldn't think twice about Levi kneeling at his feet when they went out for drinks one night and capably leading a team the next morning, this was it.

That was part of why he'd founded it. He wanted to support the kink community, but he also wanted to have a space where he could be himself.

He also, however, had to lead by example. Didn't he?

He scrolled up to read the whole letter again. That plea for a Daddy was real, even if Levi joked about it.

And that was when Saul's finger slipped. Just one little button, conveniently placed to initiate a conversation.

The chat window opened up and he could see his own text bubble with the automated text: "Have you been naughty or nice?"

It was probably fun and flirty to most people who sent it, a cute way to make an introduction. Saul froze.

There wasn't a way to take it back. That was… definitely something they should consider for future versions of the program.

But maybe Levi wouldn't notice. Maybe he wasn't even logged into that account at all.

Maybe he could just tell Levi about the error, go home, delete the whole sandbox, and forget that any of this had ever happened.

Or maybe this was his subconscious telling him that he should reach out and grab everything that he'd ever wanted.

Not just grab, but kiss and spank and torment and

soothe. Tie Levi down and not let him up until he admitted he was Saul's and no one else's.

A thousand thoughts raced through his head, pros and cons rising in waves as he tried to calculate each possible future. If Levi hadn't seen the text, maybe he had just a little bit more time to figure it out.

And if he had, well, that wouldn't be such a terribly bad thing, would it? Maybe this was a sign.

If Levi read it. If Levi responded. If Levi *wanted* this…

Levi looked up at him and smirked.

8

LEVI

Levi adjusted another setting on JewBoy3's profile. Rope play: yes. He could see Perfect-Daddy. Rope play: no. He went away.

If he put it back and deselected the list item just above, puppy play, PerfectDaddy disappeared. But if he deselected *both* of them, PerfectDaddy was back.

It was maddening. He felt like he was getting closer, but there didn't seem to be a rhyme or reason to it.

It didn't help that his own perfect Daddy was just an illusion, too.

He could tell that Saul was interested. The man watched him constantly. He smiled indulgently when Levi was being ridiculous. His eyes grew round when Levi moaned over his food. And when he thought Levi wasn't looking, he devoured him with his gaze.

It had been a perfect evening, a beautiful oasis from reality. If they didn't find the bug, he might be able to extend it a little into the morning and volunteer to come back in. But then it would have to end.

There had been a couple of times where Levi had even thought Saul was going to say something. Like when he'd wiped the accidentally-on-purpose blob of whipped cream off his nose. With a napkin, unfortunately.

But he'd given him the lovey Daddy face, the one that felt like magic swirling all around them.

It had made him start to hope for more. It had made him hope that Christy was right.

Levi clicked determinedly through another few settings and let the outputs run. When he asked for the full list of compatibilities on the back end, he could see a couple hundred more matches, but he wasn't sure he had all of the distance settings the same. Ugh.

Maybe Levi should just ask Saul out.

Or maybe he needed to accept that Saul didn't want what he did.

God, that would be so disappointing. He'd gone into this looking for an enjoyable few hours with his crush. The problem was just that it had been better than he could have imagined.

He'd noticed a new expression on Saul's face today. He called it indulgent Daddy.

That had to mean something, didn't it?

He'd tried so many times before with other guys, but they usually found his exuberance annoying. Or they expected it from him all the time.

Saul seemed to appreciate his silliness as well as his

seriousness. They obviously worked well together when they were planning projects. He was pretty sure that the attraction between them was real.

Maybe Saul didn't want a boy. That was probably it. Levi knew that he was a Dom from the casual way these things were mentioned around the office when one worked for a kinky app, but he'd never mentioned being a Daddy Dom.

Or maybe he just didn't want Levi.

That would suck. Levi blew out a breath as he clicked through another combination of attributes and watched the outputs. Click on one, PerfectDaddy was there. Click on another, poof. He was gone.

Story of his life.

Something flickered in the background and he listlessly switched windows.

It was a chat window, which bubbled up with a message: "Have you been naughty or nice?"

He knew that was the auto-response for the Santa letters. But it was from PerfectDaddy. Written to his JewBoy1 account. How could that…?

It took him a moment to understand what was happening, and then his brain went around in little circles chanting *OMG! OMG! OMG!* Because *Saul was writing to him.*

He looked up and found Saul looking stunned and maybe a little wary. His eyebrows knit, but broody Daddy was one of his favorites, too.

Levi smirked. He couldn't help it. Saul was going to be his Daddy. He could feel it.

There were two buttons for "Naughty" and "Nice," but he ignored them. He typed quickly in the chat box.

Hi Daddy!

I've been very nice. The best boy ever.

He looked up eagerly. Saul was looking all serious and sexy while he read.

Levi started to get nervous when he didn't respond. Surely he'd read the reply at least a dozen times.

Slowly, Saul's hands lifted to the keys. He typed something and there was an answering flash on Levi's computer.

No, I think you've been very naughty.

Oh, yes please! But wait. Was that good naughty or bad naughty? Levi's heart felt like it would beat out of his chest.

He watched Saul, but his face revealed only an intense concentration. What the hell did that mean?

He took a gamble and tapped out a reply. Go big or go home, he supposed.

Maybe I deserve spankings.

He held his breath as he sent it off and waited for Saul to respond. And waited. And waited.

Finally Saul looked up and met his eyes. Whatever he'd been thinking about solidified into something fiery and sure.

"Then I guess you'd better get over here. Shouldn't you, boy?" His low alto voice cracked on the last word and Levi had never heard anything sweeter.

He practically tripped over his chair in his rush to get out of it.

Saul, completely composed, took a few long strides across the room and sank down on the middle of the couch. It only took the slightest nod for Levi to dive over his lap.

The stuff in both of their pockets was digging into his thighs and belly, and the leather-y stuff in the couch smelled funny when he pressed his face to it.

But it was perfect because it was real. So much better than anything he could have imagined.

Saul was going to spank him in his *office.* Saul was running soothing hands over his limbs, straightened him out from his awkward dive and putting him right where he wanted him.

"You want this?" Saul asked, voice husky.

"Please." The word *Daddy* was on the tip of his tongue, but he didn't quite dare. *Daddy* was special and sacred. He'd typed it in the chat, but that had been a thoughtless response. He needed to know that Saul wanted it too.

Right now, he would take this fantasy-come-to-life and enjoy every moment of it.

"What's your safeword?"

"Red-yellow-green," he breathed in a rush. He felt like he would shake out of his skin.

Saul's soothing hands traced down his back. Over his ass. Tingles raced through him, leaving shining trails everywhere Saul touched.

This was really happening.

Right in front of those full-length windows where

their reflections were overlaid with the sparkling stars of the city night.

Levi watched himself, cast against the darkness. He looked horribly undignified, stretched out over the couch in another man's lap. Saul was clearly in control, their positions unmistakable for anything but the act that was about to take place.

Heat washed through him. He'd been dreaming of this forever.

The first swat came down gently and he closed his eyes. It was hardly a blow, but Saul soothed it away anyway. Because Saul was taking care of him.

The next two fell harder, sending little sparks of pain dancing through him.

"You've been very naughty today, haven't you?" Saul's voice held that perfect mixture of affection and command.

Two more blows fell in quick succession, leaving him grunting.

"Yes. Sorry. So naughty," he agreed eagerly. Anything to get more.

The intensity increased, pain arcing through him in a glorious swirl of heat. "You've been teasing me. Making me watch those pouty lips and big innocent eyes."

Saul liked his eyes? And his lips? He moaned.

A soothing hand massaged his ass and Levi wished like anything that Saul would have taken down his pants first. He wanted that graceful, slender hand on him with nothing between them.

"Please," he whimpered. "Please more."

Saul struck four times in quick succession, each one landing before the last had been absorbed. Levi twisted, into it, away from it, seeking more of that glorious tangle of agony and desire.

He panted as Saul teased his stinging flesh, wriggling to get more friction on his cock.

"Stop that," Saul gave him another sharp tap. "You'll come when I say you can come."

Oh, *fuck* that was hot. Glorious need flashed through him, welling up in his dick until it was close to exploding.

"OK. When you say... OK, please."

Saul chuckled again. It was such a throaty, indulgent sound. Levi wanted to hear it all the time.

He had to open his eyes to the reflection in the glass. To see the muscles bunch in Saul's arm. To see the blur of his own face that he knew was damp with tears. To see Saul's satisfaction as he took him apart so masterfully on that uncomfortable corporate couch.

If Levi thought Saul would go easy on him after that, though, he was wrong. Saul set up a bruising pattern, each slap painting over the last like a watercolor, growing and fading and blending into a perfect landscape of pleasure.

"You've been asking for this all day, haven't you?" Saul bit out without slowing his arm. "Asking me to punish you in my office. Right in front of the windows where everyone can see what a naughty boy you are."

A hoarse scream tore from Levi's throat. He was

beyond words, but he nodded. That was exactly it. Exactly what he'd wanted, even when he hadn't admitted it to himself. And Saul was giving it to him.

"Don't come," Saul reminded him with that confident, perfect cruelty.

"K. Please. I… please."

The wash of pain slipped away from individual strikes into a haze of sensation. He was rocking again now, trying to chase Saul's hand and humping against the empty air before him. Sounds pushed through his lungs, deep and gasping.

His eyes slipped closed, everything blending together then focusing into a tiny point. Saul. Pain. Obedience. Saul.

He was so close. Right on the edge of something magnificent.

"Come, boy."

On the next slap, everything rushed through him like an earthquake, shaking him from his moorings. Need and pain and care all coursed through him, mingling into beautiful fragments and a glorious whole.

"Saul!" he sobbed. Then softer, "Saul," as the sharp strikes became gentle taps and he rode the final, shivering waves of pleasure.

It wasn't the word that he wanted to say, but some small, nervous part of his brain managed to hold it back. Having a Daddy was something special and sacred. Until he knew what Saul wanted, he'd just have to imagine it.

But it was so easy to imagine.

Long caresses down his back left him floating. Warm and safe, with Daddy to take care of him.

"Come up here, boy."

Levi barely opened his eyes as Saul guided him. There was a brief, awkward tangle of limbs, and then he was chest-to-chest with Daddy, knees to either side, and breathing in the spicy-sweet fragrance at the base of his neck.

He wanted to memorize that smell. To take the soft feel of cotton on his cheek and the downy brush of Saul's curls against his forehead and just breathe them into his lungs to keep forever.

"Good boy. Such a good boy." Daddy murmured. He ran long paths down Levi's back, calming and caressing him. "Such a good boy."

By the time he floated down, his pants had that clammy-sticky feeling that was only going to get worse as the cum dried. He should probably take off his underwear and clean up. He didn't want to move though.

Unless he could get Daddy to remove his underwear for him.

He rocked against him hopefully, and was surprised for a moment when he didn't feel an answering bulge in Saul's jeans. Kind of a soft mound, but not an erection. His muzzy head supplied the fact that Daddy didn't have a biological dick, or maybe he did but it was different or… whatever. That was something he could figure out later.

The point was that it wasn't a sign of disinterest, just the way Saul's body was.

He rocked against him again.

"You're a needy little thing, aren't you?"

He loved how Saul called him little, even though he clearly towered over the other man. He knew that his own body issues had nothing on Saul's, but he always thought of himself as much smaller than he actually was.

He lifted his head to look down at Saul. Between sitting on his lap and Levi's longer torso, it was impossible not to. But when he tilted his head to the side, he felt more the right size. "Yep. Very needy. I've been waiting for this for sooooo long."

Saul looked him over seriously, like he was trying to figure him out. He looked a little wary, too.

Whatever Saul was thinking, he didn't want to hear it. This was supposed to be lovey Daddy. Or adoring Daddy. At least not worried Daddy.

Saul sighed.

Oh. That was a very bad sign. Levi was too pushy and flirty when he should have just let things go. This was what always happened eventually. Some nice Daddy would pick him up for an evening or a week or a month, and then drop him when he got to be too much.

And now he'd made a fool of himself in front of his boss, begging for spankings and coming in his lap.

He'd forgotten for a minute that this wasn't real.

That this wasn't Daddy swooping him up into a perfect romance, but an ill-advised office flirtation.

He tried to scramble away, but Saul dragged him back in, one hand hard at the back of his neck and the other on his shoulder. "Settle," he commanded.

Levi tried to, but every muscle in his body screamed for him to run away. To hide in some corner and never show his face again. Which was going to make coming into work on Monday really shitty.

Saul ran another hand down his back. But now it felt jarring instead of soothing. He didn't want Saul's pity. He'd gotten that from more than enough Daddies.

Saul cupped his face, stroking one thumb from just above his lip around to his chin. Tremulously, he met his eyes.

Saul studied his face, but it wasn't any look that he recognized. "I've always wondered what your beard would feel like."

That was a good thing, right? It wasn't really an answer. More of a non sequitur. But it was something. It proved that Saul had been thinking about him, too. "How does it feel?"

"Soft. A little bit scratchy."

Levi realized then that Saul probably couldn't grow a beard, or at least not yet. He had one transmasculine friend with a full, bushy beard and another who complained that he could only grow three hairs at a time. Was that something Saul was worried about?

Saul stroked around his lips again with both

thumbs now. Touching him like he was something fragile and special.

Levi closed his eyes. If this was really just one evening, he wanted to enjoy it to its fullest. To pretend, just a little longer, that he had a Daddy. That his office crush might turn into something more.

He only wanted to be a little greedy, he promised himself. He wouldn't ask for more than what Saul wanted to give him.

And if Saul wanted to forget this ever happened, which seemed increasingly likely, he'd go along with it. Because they still had to work with each other.

Though that reminded him… "Do we have to get back to debugging now?" He scrunched up his nose. He really, *really* didn't want to look at the screen. Especially if it meant wasting a single second that he could spend in Saul's lap.

Saul grinned at him. "Oh, I was about to tell you that. I found the error." Adoring Daddy was back. Was that a good sign? Maybe whatever Saul had been worried about was just for the moment. After all, this had happened pretty quickly and with minimal discussion.

It took a moment for the words to penetrate. "Wait, what? When was that?"

Saul smirked. "About three minutes before you tried to convince me that you'd been a nice boy all day."

"So, it's done? I mean, do we need to fix it?"

Saul ran his fingers through Levi's hair. Such a little touch, but it seemed like everything.

"Nope. Already did. It was the new color scheme. Apparently Jazz was shifting the output ranges around at the last minute and the percentages had some gaps between them. The code was fine otherwise, as far as I can tell. Twelve hours of investigation and twelve seconds to fix it."

"Huh. So do I have to go home now?" If there was anybody out there listening, Santa, God, the Prophet Elijah, or little green aliens, please let him have more of this.

Saul chuckled. "I think we can stay here a little longer."

Levi snuggled back into Saul's arms. Maybe he could stay this way forever, with Daddy gently stroking his hair. When he rested his head a bit on Saul's shoulder and the rest on the back of the couch, they fit just perfectly together.

He could even watch Daddy hold him in the window, with the city lights shining around them like candles.

9

SAUL

Saul pressed a kiss to the collar of Levi's shirt, more a brush of his lips, really. His boy was snuggled against his chest, dark hair soft against his cheek. Levi was rubbing little patterns against his skin, just under the hem of his shirt, and it made him feel warm everywhere.

He still wanted to be closer.

God, holding him like this was better than he ever could have dreamed. Levi, his sweet, silly boy, was finally in his arms.

Saul hardly dared to breathe lest he scare him away. Or let the reality of the situation come crashing through.

Now that he'd had a taste, could he help but want more?

Levi had been stunning laid out over his lap, his throaty cries holding nothing back. Everything about the scene had been exactly what he would have expected from the naughty, needy sub. He'd arched into Saul's hand, chasing the next strike. When Saul had told him not to come, it sounded like his moan had been ripped from his soul.

Having him here hardly seemed real.

Saul was still as horny as hell. It was impossible not to be with Levi finally, finally in his arms. But this wasn't about him. He often didn't do anything sexual in his scenes. Even with his exes, it was more the rush of Dominance that sent him soaring.

If the JewBoy1 account was to be believed, the spanking today was just the beginning. He could see that Levi was an exhibitionist. Just mentioning the window had gotten him panting, though the likelihood of anyone seeing from this height at this time of night was almost nil. The idea of it was tantalizing, though. There were so many places that Saul would love to show Levi off.

It still amazed Saul that Levi hadn't been snapped up by another Dom a long time ago. Or rather, another Daddy.

Saul tried out the word again in his mind. What did it mean for Levi? What might it mean for him?

If today was any indication, it was a lot of watching Levi be adorable and laughing at his antics. Taking care of his boy in small ways while Levi clapped his hands in glee or gazed at him with that besotted look.

Right now, Saul got to hold him and it filled another part of his soul. Saul had always enjoyed after-care, and Levi seemed to revel in it. After all of his bouncy energy today, he seemed content to just rest his head on Saul's shoulder. His breath was slow and even. His body still except that small patch of skin that he kept touching near Saul's waist.

Levi's hand was actually touching him. Levi *wanted* to touch him. It was amazing.

The moment seemed like a bubble, trapped outside of time and reality. A tiny, perfect sphere of sensual closeness. Just Saul and his boy.

Levi shifted a bit, and Saul realized he was probably uncomfortable. They'd been snuggling in the same position for most of an hour and Levi was still wearing his shoes. Saul was also pretty sure that dried cum in your underwear wasn't a good thing, even if most of his knowledge of the male anatomy was by hearsay.

Levi wasn't complaining, though. He just nuzzled in further.

"Are you falling asleep on me, boy?" he murmured against his ear. It would be alright if he was, but he might be more comfortable in another position.

Levi shook his head, but didn't sit up. "Not sleeping. I was looking at our reflections."

Saul shifted until he could see, and the bubble of calm popped.

There they were. Saul's feet barely touched the floor while Levi's long legs were tucked against his thighs. Levi was still a full head taller, and wide enough that most of Saul's body was hidden behind him.

It was frustrating. Not at all like he thought a Daddy and boy should look. Not that body shape was that important. But well… it still was. On top of that, they were in his office. It had been hot a moment ago, but now reality was setting in. He hadn't just broken company protocol, but done it on company grounds.

"What do you see?" he finally asked.

Levi pulled away just enough to look down at him. "A naughty boy whose boss had to punish him? And then gave him snuggles?" His face was just so open and sweet. Like he didn't have a care in the world.

Levi's lightness could always cut through Saul's storm clouds. Of course that would be all that he saw.

Then Levi's nose wrinkled adorably. Saul looked forward to hearing some silly complaint.

"I suppose we ought to talk about all of this?" Levi's eyes shone with a teasing light. How could he manage to ask such an important question, but still look naughty while he did it?

The last thing that Saul wanted to do was put all of his half-formed fears into words. But with Levi taking the flirtatious lead, it seemed somewhat possible.

"Levi, you know this shouldn't have happened, don't you?"

As soon as he said it, Levi's face fell.

Saul couldn't stand seeing that expression. "Sorry, that came out all wrong. What I meant was, I'm your supervisor. If we didn't work together, it might be different, but…" He wasn't even sure what he was going to say. Something that honored how beautiful Levi was while also apologizing for putting him in this position, and probably making it clear that it could never happen again. Without hurting Levi's feelings.

Levi cut him off with an enthusiastic shake of his head that made his wavy hair bounce. "Nope. You're not my *direct* supervisor. You don't do my evaluations. There's no conflict of interest. That's what the HR policy says."

He'd read the HR policy on this? "Technically. But I think it's a bit different when I own the company. If I even approve a temporary assistant, I can be accused of nepotism. Not to mention that if Nikhil ever left, his position would probably go to you or Christy. It would be my call to make, and then I might be your direct supervisor."

"I think that's kind of missing the point of the policy, though. I mean, if you're attracted to some-one"–he rolled his torso seductively to demon-strate–"couldn't you show favoritism without having an actual relationship? Like, what if you promoted me to get me into your bed?" He waggled his eyebrows lasciviously, like an evil villain from a silent film.

Saul laughed. Trust Levi to both have some really solid and constructive ideas and present them in the cutest, most ridiculous way possible. This was exactly why he was so perfect.

"So what would you suggest?"

"Get rid of the rule that says people can't date their direct supervisors. Change it so that *if* they're dating their direct supervisors, there have to be checks on their performance reviews and assignments. Get someone from HR and someone from another team involved to oversee areas where there could be conflicts of interest. Bring it out in the open so that you're relying on transparency instead of asking people to do the morally right thing for the good of the company at the expense of their personal happiness, or the reverse."

Somehow, during that conversation Levi had shifted back from sweet boy into competent project manager. It seemed like they shouldn't be having this conversation with their bodies still twined so intimately together, but Saul couldn't bear to let him go.

Anyway, if this really worked out, maybe he wouldn't have to. "That makes sense, but, I mean, is that a typical HR practice?"

"It is, actually. Not everywhere, of course. But companies have figured it out. There's even this thing called a loooooooove contract." He clasped his hands to his chest and batted his eyes.

"Really?"

"It more or less says that everything's consensual, puts some guidelines in place for behavior and potential conflicts of interest, and protects the company from damages if the couple breaks up."

"You've done a lot of research on this." It was oddly flattering. Amidst all of these logistics, Levi was saying that he wanted this enough to find a way to make it work.

"Well, I'm not the only employee at Cuffd with a crush on my boss."

"Wait, really?"

"Yes, and I'm not going to tell you who the others are. But if you change this policy, I'd expect at least two new relationships out of it. Maybe more."

Seriously? "There aren't even forty people in the company!"

"Yep. And they all talk about their kinks during meetings to provide input on the app design. It's like a buffet."

Saul rolled his eyes. "Alright, brat. You really think this is the ethical thing to do?"

Levi nodded solemnly. "It makes a lot of sense."

"People are still going to talk."

"People are going to cheer. I'm personally expecting a nice round of office-themed kinky memes and gag gifts."

"Ugh. You're probably right."

"I mean, they're not wrong... boss." Levi looked pointedly around the office. "Great choice of location, by the way."

"You goaded me into it, naughty boy. Though it was hot, wasn't it?"

"OMG, yes." Levi actually said the letters out loud. "I hope you know that this is basically what I imagine maybe, twenty percent of the time I walk in here. After today, though, I'll probably never be able to concentrate again."

Yeah, neither would Saul.

"Listen." Levi gave him what was probably the first serious look that day. "It's a small company and everyone knows you. They want you to be happy. They want me to be happy. Just be honest and give everyone else the same opportunity."

Huh. That was kind of sweet. And having a realistic solution to the office relationship issue was a huge weight off his shoulders.

But it also exposed the real fears that lurked underneath. The ones that said he wasn't man enough. That he wouldn't know how to navigate the complexities of gay culture. That Levi would take one look at his body and change his mind.

He wished so often that he'd transitioned when he was younger. Or that he could just skip over a couple years of this awkward in-between stage. Caterpillar metaphors didn't help.

Saul pulled Levi back against his chest, both to hold him close for a little bit longer and to give himself time to think. Levi settled in with a happy murmur.

Could it be that easy? Levi certainly didn't seem worried about anything. His hand was back to tracing patterns along Saul's waist, almost like it was comforting for him to be able to touch it.

Maybe he should just ask. They'd talked about corporate policies but not about the two of them.

He spoke into Levi's silky hair. "Is this what you want? Not just like…" He gestured vaguely at the couch and their intertwined bodies even though Levi couldn't see. "I mean, do you want…?" God, he sounded like a fool.

Levi met his eyes. He looked nervous. Like, really

nervous, not the playful shyness that he sometimes affected. "What?"

"Well, more, I guess? Do you want to keep seeing each other?"

Levi nodded, but he looked hesitant, too. Like he wanted to say something.

"Go ahead. Tell me." This was nerve racking.

"I just… well, you saw my profile, right? And so…"

"Mmm-hmmm…" Saul had a sense of where this was going.

After that stumbling beginning, the words all came out in a rush. "Do-you-want-to-be-my-Daddy?"

Saul would have laughed if Levi didn't look so sincere. It was such an adorable question, but with such meaning behind it. Like he really thought there was a chance Saul wouldn't want him.

Saul didn't want to let him down, but he had to be honest, too. "I'm not sure that I know how to be a Daddy." The hints Levi had given him when he was talking about those profiles earlier weren't enough.

But maybe what he really meant was *I'm not sure that I know how to be a man.* And that seemed to be a big part of being a Daddy.

Levi looked dejected. "Oh."

Saul hated seeing that look on his face. He hadn't meant to have his own insecurities get in the way. "No, I just meant, what does a Daddy do?"

The light came back to Levi's eyes and it was breathtaking. "Ohhhhh! Um, well, *my* Daddy would give me treats for being good. Or when I was cute. And give me spankings for being naughty. And he would have to like it when I have too much energy and want to sing Hanukkah songs all day, or at least be nice to me. And"–some remembered hurt flashed across his face–"not get upset if I talk with other people."

Saul had been expecting the first few comments, more or less. But the last one looked like it came from a place of real rejection.

"Did one of your exes tell you that you couldn't talk to other people?"

"I mean, not quite. He just said that I flirted with everyone. He was OK with me hanging out with women most of the time, since at least he believed me that I was gay. But he wasn't the only one. I've been on dates before and run into a friend, then had the date tell me I was cheating on him or something."

"Because he thought you were flirting?"

"Yeah. I mean, sometimes I do flirt with everyone. But it's just fun. Not like with you. That's totally different."

Saul pondered that. "I think I saw something different today. But it was, well, very subtle."

"Yeah, well, I wasn't really trying to flirt with you."

"Boy, if that wasn't flirting, I don't know what it was."

Levi hmphed. "I mean, yes, I was flirting." He ran his fingers along the hem of Saul's t-shirt. "But really I was just, well, I wanted to pretend that you were my Daddy for the day. You know, while we were still getting work done. I was trying not to be greedy," he huffed.

That was so sweet it was almost heartbreaking.

"I think that your issue isn't flirting. It sounds like it's about trust. You want a Daddy who will let you flirt with other people, but know that you don't mean it. Right?"

Levi nodded. "That's right. Is that OK?"

"I would never want to dim your enthusiasm. It's clear to see that you love people. Anyone who's jealous of that probably has a lot of their own issues that they need to work on."

Not that Saul didn't have mountains of issues. They just weren't *those* issues. Levi was beautiful when he shone.

"Thank you. I don't think I've ever had someone understand that." Levi was still worrying at Saul's shirt, though.

"Is that all? I don't understand why anyone wouldn't want you."

Levi laughed, but it sounded forced. "Oh, there are a million reasons. Too pushy. Too tall. Too playful when I'm supposed to be serious. Too confident when I'm supposed to be submissive. Too selfish and greedy. You'll see."

"Wait, someone said all that to you?"

"Not someone. Everyone. Like, the whole league of Daddies. I'm not really boy material." He announced it like it was a done deal.

"I don't understand. I don't think you're pushy. Or greedy." Saul stroked the lines around Levi's mouth, exploring the texture of his bristly-soft hair. He couldn't stand seeing that frown.

Levi stared at him. "You just said I pushed you into spanking me. Like, a second ago."

Oh. Huh. "Alright, but… you were playing."

"I know. Playing when I was supposed to be serious." He sounded defeated.

Saul tried to remember what else had been on that list. *Too tall.* And fuck, but hadn't he been thinking that a minute ago? Not that Levi was too tall, but that Saul was too short… which probably would have amounted to the same thing. For Saul, height was all tied up in gender identity and masculinity, but he couldn't believe that someone had been superficial enough to tell Levi he was too tall to date. Assholes.

Alright. Better not to touch that one.

"And I don't see you as selfish or greedy at all. I can't even imagine it."

"You called me needy. Trust me, it gets worse."

"Needy and selfish are two very different things."

Levi sighed. "Not for me."

OK. So that wasn't working. "I think you balance your playfulness and confidence very well. And… maybe you were a bit pushy, but it was charming. If you hadn't been, I don't think we'd be sitting here right now."

"Yeah?" Levi looked hopeful for a moment, but then he dropped his eyes.

Oh, God. Someone had really done a number on Levi. Or, apparently, everyone.

Saul had never realized there was such a broken-hearted boy inside that cheerful, sweet shell. He hid everything so well under his humor that Saul never would have known.

That was when he decided.

Saul might not be the perfect Daddy, but as long as Levi wanted him, he would be the best damn Daddy that he could.

He slipped a knuckle under his boy's chin, tilting his face upward. "Levi Moishe Cohen, I would be honored to be your Daddy."

Levi blinked, like he couldn't believe it. Then he started peppering Saul's cheeks with kisses. "Daddy, Daddy, Daddy!"

Saul laughed. He hadn't had any idea how good it would feel to hear those words. It was sexy and adorable, but also deeply affirming. Daddy was an inherently masculine role. Being Levi's Daddy was like a wish he'd thought would never come true. How could he do anything less than adore this breathless enthusiasm?

Levi pulled back to look at him, apparently liked what he saw, and started kissing the other side of his face. If he noticed how smooth Saul's cheeks were, he certainly didn't seem to be bothered. "Daddy, Daddy, Daddy!"

He drew back again so they could meet each others' eyes. "Saul Elias Kauffman, I would be honored to be your boy." He burst into giggles.

Saul was grinning so widely that his cheeks hurt. "You are adorable."

"Really?" He batted his eyes ridiculously, but now that Saul knew the hurt behind it, he had a whole new perspective.

His boy would need a lot of affirmation and praise, and he shouldn't have to beg for it. Saul would shower him with it. "Absolutely." He gripped the back of Levi's head and held him still. Following Levi's actions, he pressed a kiss to his forehead. "Adorable."

He moved down Levi's face to the tender folds beside his eye. He was just starting to get the faintest wrinkles, and Saul kissed those, too. "Sweet."

He kissed just below Levi's ear, making it slow and reverent, lingering to absorb his skin. "Sexy."

He touched his lips to the corner of Levi's mouth. "Fun." And the other corner. "Responsible."

He could feel Levi wrinkling his nose.

"No, I mean that. This only works because I trust you to be an outstanding project manager and responsible at work. Your serious, practical, and responsible side is just as attractive as the rest of you. It's part of what makes you a good boy." He kissed the thin tip of his nose.

He dragged his lips over to Levi's other ear. "Even though I love it when you're naughty, too." Levi shivered in his arms.

"I might have to be very naughty," Levi warned teasingly. "To make up for lost time."

"I'm sure you will."

Saul finally gave into temptation and kissed those tender lips. Levi's mouth was so soft, the perfect contrast to the prickly scruff surrounding them. His lips parted on a sigh, but Saul kept his touch light. This wasn't about sex. It was about intimacy.

When Levi blinked down at him, he looked dazed. No, awed. "*My* Daddy," he whispered.

Saul felt something settle inside of him.

"My boy."

10
———

LEVI

Levi had been waiting for hours for everyone to wake up. Even after his late night with Saul, or actually *because* of his late night with Saul, he was buzzing with energy. He just couldn't stop moving.

He showered, tidied up the apartment, did his laundry in the basement machines, ate breakfast, fixed the bathroom doorknob that was always wiggly. Since the weather was nice, he'd walked to the office and retrieved his bike, and it was still barely ten o'clock.

But that was late enough for people to be awake. He *really* wanted to call Saul, but he wasn't sure if that was a good idea. So he called Christy instead.

"Hello?" she sounded groggy.

"Oops. Are you sleeping? I can call back." Wasn't ten late enough? On such a glorious morning, it seemed like the whole world should be awake.

"No, I'm up now. Did you find the bug?"

"Yes. But guess what?"

"Your Daddy spanked your naughty butt and took you home with him?"

"Dammit. You take all the fun out of everything."

"Hang on, really?" She sounded much more alert now. "Tell me everything."

"So, I wrote these, like, fake profiles in the system, but Daddy read them, and then he brought me a candy cane mocha, and I thought it was like a sign or something, but actually he just read the letters, and then he gave me spankings."

"I understood about five percent of that. So let me get this straight. Mr. Responsible with the broody Daddy face gave you spankings."

"Yep."

"In the office."

"Yep!"

"You lucky bastard. That must have been hot."

"OMG. It *waaaassss*. He put me over his lap, like right there in the office, and just took charge. And Christy, it was sooooooo good. I even cried, and then he cuddled me for, like, two hours."

"You're still high off the endorphins."

"No, I'm high off of *I have a Daddy and it's Saul and he's perfect*."

"You're skipping right now, aren't you."

"I'm *dancing*. There's music on." He held the phone up to the speakers. Yes, it was still Hanukkah music, but he felt obligated to play it for at least a couple weeks as his own personal counter-attack on the Christmas Invasion.

"So I take it he's not there right now?"

"No," he sighed. "He said I needed to sleep." That brought back a warm glow. He'd wanted nothing more than Daddy holding him while he slept. Or maybe getting up to some other fun. But Saul had driven him home in the frigid rain, double-parked in the quiet street, and then given him a lingering kiss in the apartment lobby. He'd called him *sweet boy* and told him to get some sleep so tenderly that Levi had practically floated up to his apartment.

"And did you sleep?"

"Well, I went to bed. I was all relaxed and floaty last night, but now I have too much energy because *I have a Daddy!*"

Christy chuckled. "Well, I'm happy for you. You two both deserve it. And I think you'll be good for him."

"You think…" He hadn't really thought about being good for Saul. Well, obviously, being a *good boy* for him, but being a good influence or good partner or whatever? He just knew that they'd sparked a connection on the first day and it had only grown stronger over time. "What do you mean, I'll be good for him?"

"He carries a lot of responsibilities around. Not that you don't, but he lets his responsibilities weigh on him and I think you could help him relax. I also wouldn't be surprised if he has some concerns about his gender identity."

"Really? That's silly. He's a guy."

"You might think it's silly because most of the trans people we know transitioned a while ago, and they get read as male all the time. But do you remember when Quinn was in college?"

"Oh, yeah. It was all he could talk about. I don't think he's mentioned his transition in years, though. Like, he *is* trans, but it's not a thing."

"Well, I could be wrong, but my guess is that even if Saul's not saying anything, he's probably thinking a lot about who he is, how people perceive him, and how he fits into the world. You always knew him with a male identity, but I'm sure he's aware of how many people in his life didn't, including most of the office staff and his family."

"Huh. I guess I should have thought about that. He just seems so confident and in control all the time."

"Doms get nervous too, you know."

"Wait, really?" he teased. He'd certainly heard enough of Christy's own insecurities over the years to ever think it was easy. Dominants had to be responsible for so much stuff—which he was forever grateful for so that lucky subs like him didn't have to. "So what do I do? Should I call Quinn and ask for advice?"

"Well, I'm not trans, so I can't tell you what to do. But I'd be alert to ways that you can show him that you think of him as male all the time. Then, just ask honest questions about his body and what he likes. I'd probably check with him about sharing his trans status with your friends, though Quinn could be a good resource."

"Thanks, Christy." Everything she'd said was probably exactly what he would have told someone else, but it was helpful to have her confirm it. It felt different, too, when it was him and Saul. He didn't want to screw this up. "Any other advice?"

"This probably goes without saying, but be yourself. I've seen you try to contort yourself to be what other Daddies want, and it's always a shitty idea. He already knows you and he likes you."

"What if I'm too much?"

"Let him set the boundaries on your behavior. You'll feel better when you have rules, and you know which limits you can push and which ones you can't. But let him do his job as a Daddy instead of doing it for him."

"God, Christy. It's like you know me or something."

"Babe, you are a greedy little brat. And that's clearly Saul's thing, so live it up. I'm sure he'll keep you in line."

"Mmmmmm…" He hammed it up, dragging out the moan far past the point of decency. But the idea sent a very real shiver down his spine. That was what he needed.

"I hope you're not touching yourself right now, because I really don't want to hear it."

"Christy, would I ever do such a thing?"

"If you were thinking about Saul you would."

"Ha! Guilty. I totally would. But I'm not right now. Ohhhhh! I forgot to tell you the best part!"

"You're in chastity?"

"God, I wish. I mean, I don't wish. But, no, listen. The best part for *you!*"

"What?"

"Saul's going to talk with HR about changing the

policies about dating in the workplace. I gave him your whole spiel and he's going to talk to Javier on Monday."

"No way. Are you serious?"

"Yep. I'm getting you a flogger for Christmas. You're welcome."

"Holy shit. I should have convinced you to hook up with the CEO sooner."

"I know, right? So, tell me all of your big plans for Nikhil. I know you have them."

For once, Christy's usually cheerful voice was subdued. "I dunno. I mean… I never expected this to happen. We joke about it, but what if he's not interested? I mean, all I'm going on is his Cuffd profile from, like, three years ago. And he hasn't dated *anyone* in all that time. I don't even think he's played casually."

Levi knew all of that. Probably even a bit more than Christy did, though he'd never break Nikhil's confidence. It only convinced him further that Christy was his perfect match. She just needed a pep talk.

"Babe, he wants you. He watches you all the time. I bet he gets hard every time you challenge him in a meeting. Plus, he's a service sub. Preferably with a side of humiliation. Just ambush him at the airport and tell him he's coming home with you."

"Ha. I'll think about it. I just… don't want to mess it up." She sounded really serious. Over the years, he'd heard her worried, but this was a whole new level. As her best friend, he wasn't going to let her hold back. They supported each other this way.

"You won't. I know he's shy. And I agree that his last

Domme probably fucked him over somehow." In fact, he knew she did, though Christy had figured that out all on her own. "But you'll get it right. He needs structure." If anyone knew what that felt like, Levi did. "Be aggressive. Go out and claim him. Then get him all embarrassed and don't let him come for a week. It'll be perfect."

"I'll think about it." There was a long pause, but it sounded like she was about to say something else. Instead, all he got was a blatant topic change. "Speaking of not coming, when do you see Daddy again?"

"I'm not letting this go, you know." He really wanted her to be happy as he was, but he could accept that she needed some time to think.

One topic change coming up. "But I don't mind talking about my favorite topic in the universe if you want to listen. So… we didn't exactly plan anything. I kind of thought he'd tell me. I mean, do you think I can call him? I wanted to this morning, but I wasn't sure."

"So you woke me up instead?" Now cheerful Christy was back. They could dive into the heavy stuff later.

"Yeah, 'cause you're my bestie. And I was going to call you anyway. So, do you think I should call him?"

"I can't even believe he let you out of his sight. Unless he said he was busy, he wants you to call."

"I shouldn't, like, give him some space or anything? I won't be too greedy?"

"Remember what I said? Let Daddy set the limits."

"Right. Right! OMG I have a Daddy!" He was the happiest boy in the world, and soon Christy would be this happy, too.

"Bye, Levi." He could almost see her rolling her eyes, but she said it fondly.

"Bye!"

Levi ended the call and then stared at his phone. Would Saul really want a call from him? Was it too early? Not just too early in the morning, but too soon? It had hardly been twelve hours since they'd seen each other.

Also, Saul had said pretty clearly that he didn't know how to be a Daddy. Did that mean he didn't want to be a Daddy?

No, he'd said he would be *honored* to be Levi's Daddy. Levi had to trust that.

He found the number in his phone and changed the details from *Saul Kauffman* to *Daddy*. There. Much better.

Holding his breath, he pressed the call button. It rang.

And rang.

Should he leave a message? Call back? Text?

"Hey baby." Saul's warm voice filled his ear.

The seductive welcome was all he needed for his enthusiasm to break free. "Daddy!"

"Good morning. You sound like you're in a good mood."

"Oh, I am! I'm in a perfect mood!" Levi danced around the room, swiveling his hips. He knew he had no rhythm, but it didn't matter when so much happiness was dancing through him.

"Oh, and why's that?"

"Because you're my Daddy. Obviously."

"Well, I have to say that I woke up in a pretty good mood myself."

"Because of me?"

"Obviously." He could hear the smile in Daddy's voice.

"When do I get to see you again?"

"I believe someone requested Chinese food and movies with his Daddy on Christmas day. Isn't that right?"

"Wait, really?" Levi squealed.

"Yes, really. Your place or mine?"

"I don't care. Either one. You know…" he whispered, "that's what I was thinking about yesterday. When you called. About watching a movie on the couch while my Daddy was touching me…"

"Oh, really… And was that Daddy me?"

"It was as soon as you called me."

"Hmmmm… And did Daddy let you come?"

"Nuh-uh."

"I'll have to keep that in mind," Daddy chuckled. "And speaking of, I seem to recall a kink list on Cuffd. Was that accurate? The JewBoy1 profile?"

Levi felt himself blushing. "Yeah. That was mine."

"I was hoping so."

"Are you interested in those things, too?" Oh, please, please, please, please, please.

"We're a very close match, actually. In fact, I have a real profile on Cuffd."

Levi found himself scowling. Was it too soon to ask Saul to take it down?

"I don't actually use it for dating. You'd have seen it if you'd ever been to a marketing event with me. But it's accurate, and so's my Cuffd Communicator list. Look up SaulFromSeattle when you have a chance."

That chance was going to come about ten seconds after they got off this phone call. He would have looked it up now, but of course talking with Daddy was even better.

Plus, he wanted at least an hour to pour over every detail and imagine the possibilities. Cuffd Communicator was the spin off app that you could use for sharing your kink list. He hadn't worked on it, but it was supposed to have 600 different kinks, and you could mark them with your level of interest and experience.

"OK, Daddy. That's a terrible username, but I'm going to read it today."

"Cheeky brats get spankings. It's for marketing. And I'd like your real checklist if you have one ready. The boxes don't tell me enough about what drives you wild, what you've always wanted to try, and where your soft and hard limits are."

Part of that sounded a bit too smooth and practiced. "Daddy, was that part of the sales pitch?" Levi teased.

"Um... some of the language was." Saul laughed. "I really do want to know all of your interests and limits though, of course. And then go over every dirty detail with you."

"OK. I'll share my Google Sheet with you."

"Levi, I'm shocked! You work at Cuffd and you're using a spreadsheet for your kinks?"

"Well, it seemed weird to actually use Communicator since I work there. Plus, with my sheet, when I read about a new kink, I can just add it to the bottom. And you can put comments in it…"

"I'm not putting comments in your Google Sheet. Uh… that sounded dirtier than I expected. Alright, baby, send me your spreadsheet and we'll talk about all of those naughty little ideas you've been adding."

"Yes, Mr. Kauffman. I'll have it on your desk by the end of the day."

"We have to talk about that, too."

"We should schedule a meeting."

"Boy, you are angling for a spanking."

"This is not a deterrent. And I do want to talk about it. But do I have to wait till Wednesday to see you? That's an awfully long time." And now that he had a Daddy, he was greedy for more.

Maybe he should tone it down, though. Fight his pushy inclinations.

"Unfortunately, I need to meet a friend for lunch and then I'm looking over his portfolio as a favor. He's just in town for a few days, and this is the only time. But I'd love to see you this evening."

"Ooh! And take me dancing?"

"Dancing?"

"I just have so much happiness inside me that I want to explode. I need to go dancing."

"Well, in that case, I suppose we better go dancing. I warn you, though, that I'm pretty bad at it."

"Oh, I am too! It doesn't matter, though. I just need all of the music and energy around me."

"Are you dancing now?"

"Yep."

"To Hanukkah parodies?"

"Yes!"

"How long have you been awake, baby boy?"

"Oh, hours. Since 6:30, maybe? I did laundry and ate breakfast and even fixed this stupid door thing, and I called Christy, but not until a reasonable hour. And she said it would be OK for me to call you, so I've been *very good*." He emphasized it, just so Daddy would know.

"Levi, it sounds like you did a lot of good things this morning. But did you consider that maybe you shouldn't say anything to Christy yet?"

Levi's heart sank, all of the bubbly feelings from a moment before evaporating as he realized the gravity of his error. He'd been so careful about not sharing Christy's details with Saul, but he hadn't ever thought about it going the other way. Not only had he disappointed Daddy, but he'd potentially made things complicated for work. Or at least it would look that way.

"Shit. I'm really, really sorry. I… can I explain?"

There was a long pause. Levi felt like he was going to be sick.

"You may."

"She, uh, kind of already knew how I felt about you. Like, she realized I had a crush on you right when we started working together. She's my best friend and she was the one who encouraged me to spend more time with you yesterday. When I called her today, she actually guessed what had happened before I said it. So I guess I wasn't really thinking of it as telling her anything.

"But that's not an excuse," he continued. "I broke your trust. I should have talked to you as my Daddy and my boss and my… you know, my everything. I'm sorry."

"Thank you for telling me. Do you think she would tell anyone else?"

"She's known how I felt for almost a year and hasn't said anything. I can't imagine why she would now. And I wouldn't tell anyone else, either, unless we talked about it. I can text her to make sure." Levi's stomach was still twisting around itself. This wasn't the type of trouble he liked to be in.

"I would appreciate that. And baby, it does make sense. I would have liked a heads up, but it sounds like you trust her to keep your confidence, and I don't want to prevent you from talking with your friends. It's just complicated because we all work together."

"I know." Levi sighed. "I knew I would screw this all

up." He threw himself down on the couch. "It's OK if you don't want me any more."

"Hey baby, listen to me." Saul's voice was both stern and affectionate, that intoxicating blend that always went straight to Levi's cock.

"Yes?"

"I still want you. You didn't screw this up. You recognized the problem, apologized for it, and explained why you made a reasonable choice based on a long history with Christy. I trust you."

"I… thank you. I don't feel like I deserve it right now. Like, less than twenty-four hours and I've already messed things up."

"Hey, can we switch to a video call? I want to see you."

Levi didn't even answer, he just pushed the button and a moment later Saul's round cheeks and worried eyes filled the screen. Even on a Sunday, his hair was perfectly combed and he was wearing a black shirt with a sharply folded collar that added to his aura of power.

Levi was still laying on the couch, his phone held above him. He was sure that his hair was a total mess, spilling out everywhere.

"Hey, baby boy."

He tried to smile. "Hi."

"Tell me what you're thinking."

"I just… I always screw things up. But usually not this way. Usually I'm too… well, I told you about that already. This just makes me worried that I'm going to mess things up again. And I really don't want to disappoint you. I feel terrible."

"I didn't say any of that to make you feel terrible. And I'm not disappointed. I just needed to know what was going on."

"I know. Now I'm probably being too dramatic." He didn't feel dramatic, though. He felt sad.

Another look of irritation crossed Saul's face and Levi shrank back. "I can go. You probably have important things to do."

"No, that's just the thing. I want to be there with you, and I have to leave in about half an hour."

"You do?"

"Yes. And I'm frustrated about the timing because I need to make sure that my baby's alright, and I would rather do that with you in my arms."

"You would?"

"Who am I, boy?"

His throat caught. "Daddy?" he whispered.

"Is that a question?"

It had been, actually. But maybe it shouldn't be. "You're Daddy." He felt better just saying it.

"That's right. Now, I want you to sit up and find a way to prop up your phone so I can see you."

A command. Good. That was what he needed. He grabbed the stand he used for his tablet and returned quickly to the couch. "Is this OK, Daddy?"

"Very good, boy." Oh, God. Levi got all shivery every time he heard that voice. He wasn't sure if he was supposed to be turned on right now or not, but he totally was. Maybe they were just having a conversation, though.

"Take off your shirt."

Oh, fuck. This wasn't just a conversation. Levi whipped his shirt over his head and waited for the next instruction.

"Show me your hands."

Levi's first thought was to just present them, palm out, for inspection. But he wanted to show Saul just how submissive he was feeling. How much he needed to be guided.

He raised them to his chest, fingers loosely closed and wrists pressed together. If he were waiting to be cuffed, this was exactly how he'd present himself.

"Beautiful, boy. I want you to imagine, now, that those are my hands. That I'm going to be touching you."

"Yes, Daddy." Levi felt all of his worries start to fall away. Daddy was here and Daddy was taking care of him. Maybe he really hadn't messed everything up.

"Touch your face. As carefully as I would touch you." Daddy's voice was husky. This was adoring Daddy, looking at him like he was everything.

Levi traced along his own cheekbones, remembering how Daddy had kissed him so gently yesterday. How he'd kissed him and said such wonderful things about him.

He stroked around his lips, remembering how Daddy had followed that path over his bristly mustache and down below his chin. How Daddy said he'd been wanting to touch him there.

"Like this, Daddy?" He knew he was doing it right, but he wanted to say it. To claim Daddy as his.

"That's right, darling boy. Touch your lips. I think about your lips all the time. You're always smiling or pouting or laughing and it just makes me want to kiss you."

Levi caressed his closed lips. His skin felt so sensitive there. Even more, he loved knowing that Daddy had been thinking about him. "I like kisses, Daddy."

"I know. That's why I'll have to give you a lot of them. But right now, touch your neck. Do you see how I would explore your throat? Touch that soft place below your ears?"

Levi felt tingly all over. His hands didn't feel like they were his own any more. "Yes, Daddy."

"Now your chest. Long strokes, all the way down to your belly."

Levi nodded and complied. All of his skin was coming awake, his body singing. Saul's greedy eyes followed the path of his hands. He leaned back to provide a better view as he traced back up over his ribs.

"That's right, baby. Now circle your nipples. Lightly."

Levi grunted at the contact with the sensitive nubs. He was ready for so much more. But it was so good with Saul holding him back. With Saul controlling everything.

"Oh, you like that, do you?"

"Yes, Daddy."

"Pinch them."

His eyes fluttered shut as the sharp torment mingled with the pleasure.

"Harder. Twist them."

"Daddy…" He could hear himself moaning.

"Good boy. Touch them gently again."

He went back to the slow circles. It was even more intense now that his nipples were so aroused and tight.

"Pinch." Saul's eyes were stormy as he gave each command. Just watching the intensity on his face made Levi feel hot and loose inside. "Twist."

The new wave of pain met each command and Levi floated on it.

"Gentle now. Show me how good you can be."

Levi circled them again, no longer thinking of putting on a show but just panting and following instructions.

"Now I want you to flick them. One at a time. Flick them with your fingertips, as hard as you can."

Even though he knew what was going to happen, the sudden sting of his rough fingernail pulled a shout from his chest. God, did it hurt. He'd never done this to himself before. Never had anyone else do it.

"Daddy," he whimpered. It was so good, pulling him down to that dark, tangled place where need and pain and sex collided.

He repeated the sharp flick on the other side. "Daddy!" he screamed.

"So good," Daddy praised. "Keep going for me."

It was worse the second time, with his nipples already sore. That only made it so much better, though. He was aroused and suffering, all for Daddy.

By the time he got to the third flick on each side, it was starting to melt into a wash of pleasure. He threw his head back against the couch as he flicked again.

"Look at you, baby. We're going to need to get you some nipple clamps, aren't we?"

"Mmmmmm-hmmmmm…" he moaned. Though this was much more intense than nipple clamps. Or at least different. Clamps brought a long throbbing pain, but this was deep and bright and rough.

"Stand up, baby."

"Huh?"

"No, I didn't say to stop. I don't want you to feel anything but my fingers on your nipples for the rest of the day. Now stand up."

Levi whimpered. He felt too disconnected to comply. But he wanted to please his Daddy. Wanted to please him so much and get more of this beautiful torment.

He somehow lunged to his feet, still keeping up the erratic rhythm on his painful nubs.

"Show me your cock."

Levi was wearing sweatpants since he hadn't planned to leave the house. It took only a rough shove to get them and his briefs around his knees.

He brought his hands back to his nipples and gave them another flick, lightning shooting down his chest.

He could see, in the tiny corner of the screen, the way that his erection jumped with the motion.

But mostly he watched Daddy's face. The way that Daddy wanted to devour him.

"Stop, baby. Hands by your sides."

Levi drew in a heaving breath and pressed his hands against his thighs.

"You're so hard for me, aren't you?'

"Yes, Daddy. Just for you."

"Are you leaking? Show me. Collect it on your finger."

Just touching the bare tip of his cock sent a shudder through him. And knowing that he was going to show that pearly drop to Daddy on the phone made something dirty and wild flash through him.

"Here, Daddy."

"That's my good boy. Taste it."

He put his finger to his mouth, eyes fixed on Daddy's. The taste was briny and bitter. He wasn't a big fan of swallowing cum, but this was just a little flavor, and the act was exquisitely dirty.

He sucked, still imagining Daddy's hands. He added a second finger to his mouth and ran his tongue around them, looking at Daddy imploringly.

"Damn, baby. Look at you. You want it, don't you?"

"Please, Daddy." He didn't even know what *it* was, but it didn't matter. He wanted anything Daddy wanted to give him.

"Get the next drop. Let me see it."

This time, the slide of his slicked fingers over his tip

was gloriously worse. It was so hard not to grasp his whole shaft and jerk himself to completion. His nipples still throbbed. If Daddy told him to come, it would take only a couple of strokes.

He showed Daddy his two slippery fingers.

"Suck, boy."

He returned to the enthusiastic suction. Imagining Daddy's cock in his mouth. Or whatever the equivalent was. Imagining *Saul* in his mouth.

"That's right. God, you're gorgeous."

"Now, hands by your side. I want you to listen very carefully."

He dropped his hands, but his body was still stretched too tightly, vibrating to each of Daddy's words.

"You're going to keep doing this for me. Every time you see a drop on that beautiful cock, you're going to clean it up. Then you're going to take a picture of your fingers and send it to me. Then you're going to lick it off, just like that, imagining my fingers in your mouth."

"But Daaaaaaddy," he wailed. "I don't get to come?"

"You get to come tonight. After we go dancing."

His cock got harder, if that were even possible. "Is this… is this a punishment?"

"No, sweetheart. It's a reminder. I want you to remember who you belong to."

There was no other word but *gratitude* for that rising feeling in his chest. "Thank you, Daddy."

"Oh, you are very welcome. Now you're going to

keep doing this until either your erection goes down or an hour passes, whichever comes first."

"An hour? Daddy, I'll be hard the whole time."

"I know, baby. That's why this is your reminder. You can sit or stand, but I want every picture. If you need to safeword, tell me in a text, but stop immediately. I want you to always feel safe. Alright, sweetheart? Tell me what you're going to do."

Levi felt himself flush as he was forced to say the words back. It was so dirty, so deliciously submissive. "I'm going to just take the… the precum off my cock. And suck it off my fingers like I'm"–he almost stumbled over the words. Not because he was afraid to say it, but because it hadn't been what Daddy said earlier. Instead, it was what he wanted, and probably what Daddy needed to hear–"sucking your cock. And not touch anything else and not come. And, and, send you pictures."

"Just pictures of your fingers, baby. I don't want anything else recorded until we talk about it more."

"Okay, Daddy."

"Because I'm going to be checking my phone during my meeting."

Oh, fuck. That added another level of thrill to a scene that already had him jangling with need. If Daddy's friend caught a glimpse of those pictures, he might figure out what Levi was doing. What Saul was *making* him do.

"Good boy. I'm going to get ready to leave, but I'll be waiting for those photos."

"Yes, Daddy."

"Let me see you get started."

Levi moaned aloud as he touched the angry, red tip of his erection. God, it felt so good. His fingers were just starting to dry out, but the precum was just smooth enough to lubricate his slit.

And Daddy was still watching him with those smoldering eyes. Forcing him to drag his hand away.

The screen went dark and he fumbled to flip it back on with his trembling left hand. His fingerprint wouldn't work and he had to type in his code three times.

He took a picture. Even though you couldn't technically see the semen, it looked lewd, his two fingers outstretched and still shiny from his saliva. He fumbled through finding Daddy to compose a message and then sent it off.

Somehow, putting his own fingers into his mouth right now was more sinfully submissive than doing it while Daddy was watching him. And far more erotic than masturbating on his own.

Because Daddy had given him a task to complete, to keep himself on the erotic edge of his control for an *hour* while Daddy went on with his day. While Daddy was catching up with his friend and talking about business, he'd be here, touching himself for Daddy's pleasure. He felt wholly owned and desired.

His knees were weak and he stumbled back to the couch. His sweatpants were still tangled around his legs. His cock was flushed, the veins full as they curled around it. It looked so wicked and exposed against the couch cushions.

He had the double sensation of a mouth full of cock and suction from his own lips. He traced his tongue around his fingers, thinking of how good he could make Daddy feel.

Meanwhile, his eyes stayed on his hard dick. Another pearly drop leaked out the tip.

Oh, fuck. Daddy was torturing him. No, Daddy was beautifully, wonderfully, making him torture himself.

He swiped up the fluid. Sent the picture, which was easier this time with the message app already open.

Daddy replied back right away. *Gorgeous, baby. So good for me. I'll be thinking about you following my instructions all day.*

Another wave of desperation and desire flooded through him. He put his fingers in his mouth, sucking harder, as though by sheer will Daddy would feel his need and know how good he was sucking him.

Another drop. Another picture.

He took a note of the time. He just had to do this until… 11:35.

It was going to be a long, impossible morning.

And he was the luckiest boy in the world.

11

SAUL

S aul found a parking space a few blocks from the club. How had he ever let himself get talked into dancing? Well, it had obviously been the delight in his boy's voice that made him lose his head and promise anything.

He hated dancing. He couldn't even remember the last time he had moved his body to music.

No, that wasn't quite true. He actually enjoyed Simchat Torah, though even that had been years ago. Everyone's energy raised each other up, swooping through the synagogue as they took turns carrying the heavy Torah scrolls while dancing an endless grapevine step. It was easy to get caught up in the ecstasy of the moment, when children and elders and everyone in between all joined hands and danced the same steps. No one was too fat or old or unattractive to rejoice in the Torah. That joy and the old melodies made everyone beautiful.

He should really go back to Simchat Torah again. For the first time, he wondered where Levi went to shul and if he'd like to go with him. He hadn't been to anything except High Holiday services in almost a decade. Would Levi's shul accept their relationship? Would there be other gay guys there? Other *trans* guys? Or would Levi mind if he didn't go? He really didn't think of himself as religious.

Ugh. Add that to the list of things to worry about later.

Right now, he was worried enough about dancing. Every club he'd ever been to had felt just like middle school all over again, but with more booze. He was still the odd one out, the one who couldn't dance and clung awkwardly to the walls.

And tonight, it would be double the stress. He'd unwisely let Levi pick the venue, because he didn't have a clue. The name seemed harmless enough, *Swish*, but he should have known by that single syllable that it was going to be full of young and trendy gay men. The online reviews said it all.

It was probably going to be noisy and sweaty. Probably full of lithe, shirtless men in tiny shorts and leather daddies with hairy chests.

And Saul would be the short one, the one who kept his shirt buttoned up all the way over the t-shirt that hid his binder. Being overheated and hardly able to breathe was just something he'd gotten used to.

He'd thought his charcoal shirt and black slacks had looked sharp when he picked them out earlier, but now he wasn't so sure. He was even wearing a tie, a thin maroon one that caught the light. It would probably look stupid in the casual atmosphere. But he felt better when he was wearing it.

It was such a visible symbol of masculinity, a magical talisman that made people's eyes slide over him without giving him a second or third glance.

He wanted to look good for Levi. But he also didn't want to deal with any shit tonight.

He had to focus on Levi. That was why he was here.

If a night of uncomfortable dancing would make his boy smile, he wanted to give it to him.

Hopefully Levi would like his overdressed look and maybe even find it sexy. It wasn't too different from what he usually wore. Or what he'd been wearing this morning during that sinful phone call when Levi had watched him with such desire and longing.

Saul hadn't been able to watch those pictures come in while he drove to his meeting, but he'd poured over them later. There wasn't anything too overtly sexual about them, just two outstretched fingers. A broad palm and the other two fingers gently curled. The backgrounds were blurry and forgettable.

What made them erotic was that they'd kept coming every two or three minutes for an hour, testimony to Levi's willing torment.

A few minutes before the time was up, he'd stepped out on his friend and called Levi to praise and calm him and tell him what a marvelous, tantalizing boy he was.

Over that hour, Levi had somehow gone from desperate to floaty, his voice slurred and soft. He'd babbled quietly into the phone, happiness and dirty desires strung together like pearls with the word *Daddy* shimmering in every sentence.

Saul had told him to find a blanket and take a nap, then waited for him to settle in. On a yawn, Levi told him, "I knew you'd be the perfect Daddy."

Saul had been torn between feeling prouder than he'd ever been and regretting that he couldn't be there to watch his boy sleep.

And that, right there, was why he was going dancing.

He marched up to the door, glad that there wasn't a line yet on this damp, wintry night, and swung it open.

He handed over his ID. Thank fuck he'd gotten his gender marker changed a few months ago. The three hours at the DMV was completely worth it to not have the bouncer take a second, third, and fourth look at his clothes and face.

With a few routinized words, the bouncer returned his ID, stamped his hand, and waved him through. Around the corner, he paid the cover fee, and then he was inside.

The music was loud, but not as loud as he expected. And, probably because it was still ridiculously early, it wasn't that crowded.

He scanned the warehouse-style open space. There was a cluster of small tables with chairs at one end and another island of taller tables to stand around at the other. Most of the space was the dance floor, lit by disco lights that colored the dancers' exposed skin as they turned.

Mostly what Saul noticed was that everyone was very, very male. There was a gaggle of women in one corner, looking fierce and punky and very queer. There was a lesbian couple on the dance floor, staring into each others' eyes and dancing much slower than the beat warranted.

Otherwise, it was a very gay, masculine space. One that Saul didn't feel like he'd been invited to.

Men danced together like liquid sex on the floor, hands roving over muscular pecs, asses grinding against cocks.

There was just so much *skin.* It was like everyone was required to take off their shirts the moment they walked in the door. There were twinks with smoothly shaved chests gyrating to the heavy beat and bears with leather halters over their manly mats of hair.

Saul's eyes kept settling, though, on the older men. The ones with dark jeans and chest hair shot through with silver. The ones who looked like Daddies were supposed to look.

One was even dancing with a younger man who looked like Levi. Saul's heart skipped a beat, though it took only a second for Saul to see that it wasn't him.

Saul knew he was playing into stereotypes, which he *hated* when other people did. Most of the kink community worked really hard to let people know that all sizes, shapes, and ages could take on any role.

But a huge part of Saul still wished he could look like that.

He reminded himself again that the only one who mattered in all of this was Levi. Levi and that radiant smile it would put on his face.

He continued his perusal down the neon-lit bar. There were yet more men, lounging against the wooden counter and chatting each other up. One couple was making out while they waited for their drinks.

There were just a few bar stools toward the far end, as Saul imagined that once the audience picked up people would be fighting their way to the bar through a crowd.

Finally, he spotted Levi, perched on the second-to-last chair.

His radiant smile was turned toward another man.

Saul fought down the urge to bolt. This must be what Levi was talking about when he said that his exes had gotten angry with him for flirting. He might not even realize he was doing it. Or he might know he was flirting, but just enjoy it as a way of connecting with people.

Saul trusted him. He really did. He wasn't even jealous of the other man so much as he was… insecure. Deeply, deeply insecure.

He had the thought again that Levi should have been snapped up by some other Daddy long, long ago. But then he remembered the defeated look on his face when he explained how he'd been turned down. The anguish in his voice over the phone this morning when he'd thought Saul would call off the relationship over a conversation with his best friend.

Saul squared his shoulders and strode toward the bar. He circled around a bit because—and he knew this was stupid—the bar stools were really high and he'd look even shorter if he were standing while Levi was sitting.

He slid into the chair behind Levi and then tapped his shoulder.

Levi turned to him with a jerk of confusion that morphed into a wide smile. "Daddy!" he exclaimed. He slid off his stool and into Saul's arms, nestling between his legs and leaning in for a breathless, needy kiss.

As soon as their lips broke apart, Levi nuzzled over to his ear and spoke in a breathy whisper. "Daddy, I've been waiting for you all day. I need to come so bad and I missed you. I don't even want to dance any more. Just take me home and be with me."

Sweet fuck. Saul had never heard more beautiful words. Every time he started to doubt, it was like Levi just blew through it with his innocent need and honest desire. With Levi squirming against him and kissing his neck, whispering "Please, Daddy" in his ear with that breathy voice, he felt invincible.

Saul wrapped his legs around his boy's hips, trapping him while their groins pressed together. Levi rocked against him, his cock rubbing firmly against Saul's packer. The angle wasn't quite right for Saul to get all the sensations, but just knowing that Levi was getting off on feeling that bulge was a powerful aphrodisiac.

Levi was wearing some ridiculously tiny t-shirt which left half his torso exposed to Saul's wandering hands. He was smooth and hard in all the right places.

Levi nuzzled around to his other ear. "Daddy, you're so hot. Take me home now?"

He gave his boy a sharp slap on the ass, which, predictably, made him moan and thrust even harder.

"Settle down, boy. We came here to dance." They were the last words Saul ever expected himself to say, but this wasn't about him. It was about Levi. It was about letting Levi dance through all the happiness that apparently wanted to explode inside him.

It was also about Levi being too horny and denied to even think. To make sure that he knew that Daddy was in charge and was going to take care of him.

Even if it meant dancing.

Levi pouted at him, clearly aware of exactly how adorable he looked.

Saul brushed a kiss over his lips. "You're cute as fuck, and we're not leaving yet."

Levi wrinkled his nose and Saul had to kiss him again. "Dancing."

With a sigh, Levi turned around, grasping Saul's arms to keep them wrapped around his chest. Saul released the lock of his legs, but Levi was still cupped between them, grinding back with his ass like the naughty boy he was.

Saul had forgotten that there was another person

next to them, but Levi clearly hadn't. "Hey Neil. This is my Daddy, Saul. Daddy, this is Neil."

Saul disentangled one arm to shake hands. Neil's grip was sure and strong. He was a little older, a bit heavy-set, also wearing a button-down shirt, and, yeah, basically another Daddy-type.

"Hi, Saul. Levi was telling me all about you. I'm totally jealous."

Saul bristled. Did this dude just make a pass at his boy right in front of him?

"I know!" Levi's voice was triumphant.

"Why are all the good Daddies taken?" Neil complained.

Oh. Ohhhh. It was like tonight was trying to hit Saul over the head with his own stereotyped misconceptions.

"I'm sure you'll find your Daddy," Levi commiserated. "My suggestion? Get a sparkly t-shirt."

Saul turned Levi to the side to see his shirt. The tiny scrap of white fabric said *Daddy's boy* in glittering blue letters.

Dammit. Just when Saul didn't think Levi could be more affirming and amazing, he did something like that. It wasn't just a declaration of Levi's identity, but a public claiming of their relationship together.

"I like your shirt, baby," he whispered in his ear.

"See? Daddy likes my shirt," Levi reported to Neil. "That means it's working. I've been waiting and waiting to wear this one." He squeezed Saul's arms tighter around his chest. "I have a bunch of other ones that just say *boy* or *brat* or stuff like that, though. It really helps in a place like this."

"I don't think I could ever wear something like that. It's too… not like me. I'd look ridiculous."

Levi laid a hand over Neil's, stretching out across the bar counter. "Trust me. Buy the shirt. I thought I was too tall and awkward for stuff like this, but you kind of have to embrace the awkward and just pretend. So get up your courage and just wear it once. The Daddies will be swarming all over you."

Was that how Levi felt all the time? Like he was too tall and awkward so he had to pretend? Or did he used to feel that way and then grew into himself a bit more? He always seemed so comfortable and exuberant, but there were clearly some old wounds.

Saul wanted to sew them all up. Or perhaps the right metaphor would be to kiss them and make them all better.

Neil was still looking glum and disbelieving, so Saul spoke up. "I don't know you at all, Neil, but I have to say I agree with Levi. There's a Daddy out there for you somewhere. And you could totally grab some attention with a shirt that says *boy* on it.

"You don't need to wear a teensy scrap of fabric like this naughty boy." He pinched Levi's side, eliciting a shriek. "If you're worried about how you'll look, just get a solid black T in your regular size. The Daddies will definitely notice." He didn't know where he was coming from with this advice, since he'd been a Daddy for all of one day. But he did believe in everyone finding their match, and he knew all about using t-shirts to assert his identity.

"Oh, and one more thing. Make a profile on Cuffd."

"The kink app? Isn't that for, like, hard-core stuff?"

"Nope," Levi took over. "Fair disclosure, we work there. Well, Daddy owns it." He giggled. "But people use it all the time to just select one thing, like Daddy kink. The app will just match you with people who have similar interests."

"Wow. Thanks, guys. This means a lot to me."

"No problem. Hey, want to exchange numbers? We could hang out sometime."

"Sure."

"Great! There's this munch that I go to with lots of Daddies. And this other club has a Daddy night."

Saul let the two boys chatter, resting his head on Levi's shoulder and soaking in his bubbly excitement.

This was nice. They were tucked into a little corner away from the noise. Levi continued to stand and eventually Neil moved over to his empty chair. The bartender stopped by and Saul got an overpriced drink to nurse while he broke in occasionally to encourage Neil or whisper sexy things in Levi's ear.

When Levi eventually decided it was time to dance, though, Saul was hit by another case of nerves. What would they look like standing together, with Levi towering over him?

But Levi dragged Neil into the chaos of the dance floor with them and they danced in a loose circle.

Exactly like middle school, except Saul felt like he was part of it.

Neil was surprisingly talented, showing off dazzling moves that Levi would attempt with far more enthusiasm and far less skill. Levi wasn't kidding when he said he didn't have any rhythm, but when he couldn't do something, he only laughed harder. When particularly romantic songs came on, Levi would dance around him, holding up his fist like it was a microphone as he stared into Saul's eyes.

It was… good. Fun. Energizing, even. Levi's joy wrapped around their little circle, and since Saul knew he'd never do anything as ridiculous as what Levi was attempting, he let his body become a conduit to the music.

Maybe, he might even go dancing again.

12

LEVI

Levi danced into his apartment building, Saul following behind him in amusement. Levi shook his ass as he pressed the elevator button, glorying in the knowledge that Daddy was watching him.

"You're not danced out, babe? I thought you'd be ready to crash."

"Nope." He led Daddy into the elevator. He remembered his quip from yesterday about letting Daddy open doors for him, but as usual, he was too excited to actually follow through on it.

If Daddy wanted to make a production out of opening doors for him, he would love it. But if Daddy was letting him lace their fingers together and pull him along while Levi's body bounced in excitement, that was just as good. Daddy was coming home with him!

"What floor?" Daddy asked.

He was getting Lovey Daddy face, and he didn't even have to do *anything* to work for it.

"Four." He stifled a yawn.

"That's what I thought, baby boy. You're about to crash."

"Oh, yeah. I'm tired." He let himself wilt because Daddy's arm was around his waist, ready to catch him.

"Let's get you into bed."

"Oooh! Bed! Yes, get me into bed!"

Saul laughed again, the sound filling the elevator with warmth. "Come on, sleepy boy."

He hoped Daddy knew that he wasn't too sleepy for all of the other things they could get up to in bed. Daddy had been teasing and touching him all night. They'd danced for hours with his spontaneously-acquired new friend, and then even longer with just the two of them.

They hadn't quite made out on the dance floor, though there had been a number of steamy kisses and Levi had ground against his Daddy at every chance he could take. But even with enough space between them to let them both really move, Daddy's hand and eyes had always been on him.

He was tired, though, he had to admit. It had been a long time since he'd even stayed up this late, especially not with work in the morning.

He'd take exhaustion over missing even a moment with Daddy, though.

Levi unlocked his apartment, and instead of being pushed against the wall and taken apart with another one of Saul's hungry kisses like he hoped, Daddy just cupped his cheek. "What do you need to do to get ready to bed?"

"Orgasms always make me extra sleepy, Daddy." It was worth a try.

Daddy threw back his head and laughed, but there was still no pressing him against the wall and devouring his mouth. Drat.

"I don't think you get to decide that, do you? I'm tucking you into bed."

Awww… Any disappointment he felt disappeared into a wash of warm pleasure. Because he wanted to fuck and touch and come, but even more, he wanted Daddy to tell him that he *couldn't* do all of that and then snuggle him down into sleep.

So he dutifully brushed his teeth and did all of his nighttime things. Daddy seemed to be wandering around his living room, checking out his books and things.

That was nice. He wanted Daddy to know about him. He wanted Daddy to know *everything*.

He thought about coming out to the living room naked, which really was how he slept in the summer. But in the winter his apartment got a bit drafty with all of the damp cold and he usually wore a t-shirt and pajama pants.

He decided on honesty. Because if Daddy wanted to tuck him into bed, he wanted to be all snuggly and warm. There was something more intimate about Daddy seeing him in his favorite threadbare checkered pants and worn t-shirt than decked out for the club.

He wandered out to find Daddy checking out the Jewish section of his bookshelf.

"Hey, sweetheart." Daddy's eyes were soft.

Levi just ate up all of these nicknames. He'd never dated anyone who used them so much.

"Hey Daddy." He leaned down for a kiss.

"You're really into all this, aren't you?" Daddy indicated the shelf.

"Yep. I mean… it's kind of fascinating to me."

"What would you recommend I read? Er, nothing too complicated or obscure, but I'm kind of curious since it's that important to you."

Levi was just going to die of happiness. He didn't really care if he dated someone Jewish. And he definitely didn't care if his Daddy was a Talmud nerd like he was. But it was nice to have someone who wanted to read what he read.

"Hmmm… I'd probably start with this book of Herschel's essays. His writing is just beautiful, like he immerses himself in the moment but also makes you think. And… if you're looking for something short, maybe this book of Jewish folktales and midrash. Each one's only a page or two."

"Moral Grandeur and Spiritual Audacity," Saul read. "And *Three Times Chai: 54 Rabbis Tell their Favorite Stories."* He pronounced *chai*, the word for *life*, properly with that throat-clearing sound on the *ch*. He still looked at the cover with confusion. "Ah, because chai is 18, so three of them is 54."

"Yep."

Saul hadn't forgotten as much as he thought he had. Each Hebrew word could be read as a number, since the same symbols were used for both. Since chai had the numerical value of 18, it was considered to be a number of luck and good fortune. Three of them was just triply full of vitality and wellbeing.

"Thank you, babe. I'll look these up."

"No, borrow them." He wanted Daddy reading his books, thumbing through the same pages.

Daddy put them on the table. "Thank you. Now, let's get you into bed."

Levi led him into his room, hoping that he liked what he saw. Daddy wasn't looking around, though. He drew back the covers and Levi felt all melty inside.

Levi climbed in and stuck his feet under the blankets, pampered and delighted. "Cuddles, Daddy? Goodnight kiss?" He loved asking, just because he could. Even though Saul was still wearing shoes, he was sure he would get some of the doting attention that he couldn't get enough of.

"Not yet, baby boy." Daddy pulled up the desk chair to the side of the bed. "I believe I heard about something that makes you very tired."

It took a minute for him to connect all of the dots. Daddy looked down at him, all sexy and commanding in his shirt and tie, while Levi was stretched out in front of him. His heart began to beat faster.

"Take out your cock."

Oh, God. This was what he needed.

He'd known that Daddy was a Dom. He'd hoped that Daddy would want to take care of him. But nothing could have prepared him for this exquisite blend of adoration and control. He *craved* it.

With eager hands, he pulled his PJs down just far enough to reach his dick. There was something both dirty and tender about being asked to play with himself while Daddy "tucked him into bed."

He was already half-hard from the phone scene this morning and all of the teasing at *Swish*. Even brushing his teeth had barely decreased his arousal when he sparkled with the knowledge that Daddy was in his apartment.

He could feel his shaft firming up again, driven by just the thought of Daddy's eyes on him. "Now what, Daddy?"

"Put on a show for me, naughty boy. Drive me crazy with wanting you."

Well, if Daddy wanted a show… two could play at this game.

Levi ran a hand under his shirt, stroking his belly. He wanted to come, but he wanted Saul wild for him, too. Hopefully wild enough to forget whatever plans he had and climb on top of him, pressing him into the bed.

But Daddy just watched him with a devouring intensity.

Levi reached his nipples and let out a gasp. They were still sore and bruised from earlier, a completely different sensation from the initial pain. A kind of deeper, throbbing ache that took only a touch to light up.

"Pull your shirt up. Let me see."

He obeyed.

Daddy circled one abused nub with a soft finger, sending sparks through him. "Are they sore?"

Levi nodded. "Yes, Daddy."

"Good boy."

Levi felt his cheeks warm under the praise and careful scrutiny.

"Be gentle with them now. We need to take care of you." He withdrew his hand.

Was there anything about Daddy that wasn't perfect? He knew, now, that Daddy wasn't going to jump on him and fuck him into oblivion. Whatever happened next was going to be much, much better.

Levi ran his hands back down his bare chest, hoping that Saul liked his skinny frame and little pouch of a belly. Every look, though, said that Daddy couldn't get enough of him.

He glided around the base of his cock, teasing himself and teasing Daddy, then finally took it in hand.

He stroked himself, not furiously fast or languorously slowly, but just the way he would if he wanted to come.

One hand hooked around his shaft, setting up a sensual rhythm. With the other, he cupped the head, his thumb brushing over the frenulum. His hands were a little rough, without any lubrication, but that worked for that soaring feeling of following commands.

In only moments he was gasping, his hips starting to arch up. "Like this, Daddy?"

"Gorgeous," Daddy murmured. His own breath was coming out faster, but his control was absolute.

And fuck, the way that he still wore that perfectly knotted tie while he leaned over Levi's panting, exposed body was an endless thrill.

"Keep going, sweetheart. Tell me when you're going to come."

Oh, yes. He could do that. He'd been practically on the edge all day. He stroked a little faster, dug his thumb in a little harder to that place just under the head that drove him wild. "Close, Daddy."

He wanted it so much. That tide was swelling inside him, and he was going to crash against the shore with Daddy's hungry eyes on him. One little word was all it would take.

"A little more, baby. Just like that."

Oh, fuck. He was so close. His hands had never felt as good as they did when Daddy directed him. "Daddy… need to come!"

Daddy's face was beautiful, his eyes dark with lust as he watched Levi work his shaft.

"Please, Daddy!"

"Keep going for me, baby."

"Daaaaddyyyyyy…" He couldn't keep his eyes open. His head thrashed back and forth. He was going to explode. He wasn't going to make it.

"Hands off," Daddy barked sharply.

It took him a moment to even understand the words. He needed to come. Needed it like he needed air.

Forcing his hands down to the sheets was like fighting against a heavy weight. It was horribly beautiful, leaving him open and needy and gloriously owned.

Daddy stroked a single hand down his heaving chest. "Good boy. So good for me."

"Daddy," he whined. "Do I have to sleep like this?" Because he would. Anything that Daddy asked of him. Even, or maybe especially, falling asleep hard and aching.

But that wasn't going to stop him from trying to beg his way out of it first.

Daddy lifted one of his hands and dropped a kiss on his fingers. "No, baby boy. I'm not done playing with you."

"OK, Daddy." He opened his eyes now. God, he couldn't get enough of this man.

Daddy stroked his hand down the center of his chest again, calming him until his breath was smooth.

"Do you have lube around here?"

"Second drawer."

Daddy kept his hand on his chest while he retrieved it, then turned one of Levi's hands face up to squirt a blob of the cool liquid onto it.

Levi maintained the position, waiting for the next command.

"Warm it with your hands."

He complied, though the anticipation was killing him. He didn't *care* if it was cold, not when a few quick strokes would send him into orbit.

Daddy leaned over to give him one sweet kiss. "So good for me," he whispered against Levi's lips before tracing a path down to his ear. "Now touch your cock like it's something holy."

Like it was *holy?*

What did that even mean? His cock was fun. It was aching right now. And unquestionably owned by Daddy, as Saul had already proved over and over. But holy?

He reached down with both hands, but Saul made a gentle noise of disagreement before he even touched it. "Slower. With reverence. Like… Shabbat, maybe. Show me that you are part of creation. Let me see that you're my perfect angel and that every part of you was created just for me."

That spoke to him. He thought about Shabbat, the holy overlaid on the mundane, a moment out of time. An opportunity to rest and take delight.

The idea that all humans were created in God's image, that he had been created both for toil and for joy. That this ecstasy that he was creating with Saul was part of the delight of creation.

Daddy definitely understood Judaism better than he thought he did. That thought warmed him, too.

Pausing first to breathe, he touched himself.

Daddy hummed with approval.

Levi stroked with loose fingers, noticing every

sensation. His hands acquired new depth, like he could feel his fingerprints on his heated skin through the slippery lube. His cock was a landscape of sensations, so sweet and powerful that he almost wanted to cry.

That led to a slow, dreamy session, his muscles confused as to whether they should be languid in relaxation or strung tight with arousal. He heard himself whimpering but it was far away.

At some point, Daddy stopped watching the hypnotic movements of his hands, and they just looked into each others' eyes, sharing wordless truths.

He was slipping under. Feeling glorious and reborn, like he was part of the world as it flourished into being.

When Daddy finally told him to stop, his hands trembled.

He could have slept after that, his balls so full they throbbed in agony but his head light and hazy.

But then Daddy kissed him, long and slow and sweet, easing him back from the edge and awakening new sensations. His only thoughts at first were *Daddy* and *mine* and *peace*, emotions more than words.

Until Daddy started thrusting his tongue into his mouth like he was fucking him, and his hips left the bed of their own accord. Daddy had already given him so much, but he still wanted more.

Finally, Daddy pulled back with a glint in his eye and a teasing voice. "Poor sweet baby. You've been so hard and needy all day, haven't you?"

"Yes, Daddy," he agreed helplessly. He was wrung

out. Completely owned. He hoped to always be this perfectly helpless and cared for in exactly this way.

He couldn't help but be curious, though, about whatever had brought out that Dirty Daddy face.

"I bet you could come so fast, couldn't you? Once Daddy told you to?"

Levi's still-slick hands twisted into a knot. Because Daddy called him *baby* and *boy* all the time, but that was only the second time he'd called himself *Daddy*.

"I'm so close," he whimpered.

"In that case, show me how you come for me. You have one minute." Daddy looked at his watch. "One. Two. Three. Four…."

He reached nine before Levi made sense of his words. His hands flew to his cock.

"Fourteen. Fifteen. Sixteen."

Levi jerked himself frantically, palming his oversensitive head and massaging his balls. He was moaning, his mouth open and breathing ragged.

Daddy just kept counting down the time in that deliciously superior voice. "Twenty-five. Twenty-six."

Levi was an inferno. His whole focus narrowed to his erection and his goal and watching Daddy's face.

"Thirty-one. Thirty-two." This was another side of Daddy, the commanding Dom who liked toying with him.

He'd thought he could make it. He'd even thought this would be easy. But with the stress of knowing he might not come, of being certain that Daddy wouldn't let him go a second extra, he couldn't quite get there.

Pleasure raced through him, yet he teetered on the edge of the abyss.

"Daddy!" he begged, though he wasn't sure what he was begging for. Daddy's touch? Or his exquisite denial of it? "Pleeeeeease, Daddy!"

"Thirty-nine. Forty. Forty-one."

He moved faster, urged on by the time limit and Daddy's intent stillness as he watched Levi's hands. Levi shifted his gaze as well, curling up his neck and trying to bend his knees which were still trapped by the blankets and his pajama pants.

"Fifty-three. Fifty-four."

His cock was red and angry. His hands moved in a blur. He wasn't going to make it. He was just going to *die* like this, full of need and pressure and the inexorable, merciless count down.

"Oh, Daddy…" he moaned. He wasn't going to make it, but Daddy would still catch him. He jerked himself again, squeezing tightly around the head.

"Fifty-seven. Fifty-eight."

When he came, it almost surprised him, cum spurting out so hard that it hit his neck. He cried out as he crashed against the bed, his hips arching almost against his will.

Then the whole world exploded around him like a supernova, obliterating everything but his pleasure-wracked body and Saul's voice speaking those final numbers. Dark and light, galaxies and space, all flinging him outward and inward to the universe.

He kept stroking as his orgasm passed through him,

the aftershocks shaking something loose inside him and leaving him cracked open and also whole.

Daddy shifted onto the bed, still sitting up with his feet on the floor, and cuddled him to his chest.

"So good for me, sweet boy," Daddy whispered against his sweaty hair. "You were gorgeous. I knew you could do it."

He clung to Daddy's back, stroking over his muscular shoulders through the thin fabric and digging in with his fingernails.

He needed Daddy even more now than he had a moment before. Needed to be held close and tight. Needed to make Daddy feel this beautiful haze of pleasure so that they could be one together.

"Daddy? Can I touch you? Need you, Daddy." He kissed Daddy's neck hungrily, trying to touch all of him at once. He slipped a hand between the buttons on Daddy's shirt, only barely remembering to keep his hand lower on his belly instead of higher on his chest. Frustratingly, all he felt was a layer of cotton shirt.

"You have me baby, but tonight is your night. Just for you."

He understood that, but still he wanted. He craved. His body was a rushing river of ecstasy and joy, and there was nowhere for it to go except back to his Daddy. "Just for me, can I make you feel good, Daddy? Please?"

"We both have work tomorrow, baby boy. And it's late. I need new clothes for tomorrow."

"Just wear these again. Pretty please?"

"Look down."

He was coming out of his ecstasy-soaked state, but he still didn't want to be apart. He pulled back just far enough to see the white streaks on Daddy's shirt, glistening and already turning crusty.

"OK, maybe not."

They laughed together.

"I've kept my sweet boy up too late." Daddy slowly eased him down onto the blankets. Saul slipped off his soiled shirt and used it to wipe Levi down with tender strokes. "Is this clean enough or should I get a wash cloth?"

"This is fine, Daddy. I'll shower in the morning. And I kind of like it for the memory."

Daddy kissed him again. "I do, too, baby." He drew the covers up around him, tucking them in around his shoulders.

All at once, his exhaustion hit him, curling around him like the blankets. He reached up sleepy, cuddly hands. "Can you stay a little longer?"

"Until you fall asleep," Daddy promised. "Do I need to do anything special to lock the door?"

"Nuh-uh. Locks by itself when you close it." But he still liked the idea of Daddy keeping him safe. If Daddy needed a key, he would have told him where it was.

Daddy took one of his hands, tangling their fingers together.

He wanted to stay awake. He didn't want to miss a second of this.

But he was warm and sated, completely relaxed. He

turned on his side, the way he usually slept, and Daddy kept a hold of his hand.

"Night, Daddy."

"Night, baby boy."

Daddy's lips on his forehead were the last thing he remembered.

13

───────

LEVI

Levi awoke before his alarm, feeling curiously alert even as his body wanted to sink into the mattress. He felt achy, like his muscles had been over-used, yet alive.

It only took a moment for the last two days to come rushing back to him. He settled back into his blankets and let the memory of last night spin around him in a bubble of contentment.

The way he'd felt dirty and adored while Daddy devoured him with hungry eyes. How Daddy had forced him to stop touching himself, making him cry out as agony and rapture intertwined.

The most beautiful part of it hadn't been the sensation, though, but the way that Daddy made him imagine himself. The way that Daddy saw all the parts of him. Where other people he'd been with relied on physical stimulation—and many of them were pretty good at it—Daddy got inside his *mind.*

God, he was a lucky boy.

He even lingered over the sweet kisses Daddy had pressed to his forehead as he said goodnight and reminded him that they both had to work in the morning.

Which was, unfortunately, now.

Well, maybe not unfortunately. Because work meant he got to see Daddy again, striding through the hallway or leading meetings in his perfectly cut suits.

Work also meant that Levi couldn't act like Saul was Daddy. Which was going to suck.

He hadn't been kidding when he'd said he wouldn't be able to think about Daddy's office without remembering that spanking.

Eventually Levi rolled out of bed. His limbs still felt loose and languid. His nipples were still sore from what had to be some kind of record for the sexiest phone call ever.

He stepped into the shower and scrubbed himself efficiently. Daddy hadn't *told* him not to touch himself. But he thought that Daddy would like it.

He considered what Christy had told him about not doing Daddy's job for him and holding himself back, but this was kind of the opposite. Giving over that control to his Daddy was exactly what he'd dreamed of.

Given his endless state of arousal yesterday, he rather thought Daddy would approve.

He dressed carefully in the crimson shirt that Christy said looked good on him and grabbed a protein bar to eat while he got his bike out.

The weather was still frigid and blustery, but it seemed to sparkle with a clean freshness today, like the sun might peek out soon. Knowing that he'd be arriving a bit early, and that Daddy most likely would too, made him pick up the pace.

Following his usual habit, he chained his bike to the pole outside his favorite coffee shop. The little cafe was unusually packed today. Christmas shoppers? Early travel plans? Who knew?

He found his way to the back of the line, using the time to read down the menu. He wasn't sure what he should order. A candy cane mocha delight for himself, obviously. And that nasty gingerbread sludge for Christy. But should he get something for Daddy? Er, Saul? Was that overstepping some sort of boundary?

He rocked back and forth as he pondered. He was certain he could be completely professional while bringing his CEO a coffee. Hell, he was buying Christy one and hadn't even thought twice about it.

But on the other hand, how would people see it once they knew what was going on? Or even now? He wasn't sure he could keep every trace of adoration and desire off his face if he thought he weren't being observed.

So maybe he shouldn't do it. They really should have talked about work boundaries last night while they were running through their kink limits.

Levi was almost at the front of the line. Dammit. This was why he needed a Daddy, so that he didn't have to make difficult decisions like this.

He almost laughed to himself at the absurdity of the thought. Whipping out his phone, he waved for the person behind him to go first.

"Hey baby boy."

Mmmmm… He didn't think he'd ever get sick of hearing that greeting.

"Hi, Daddy! Are you at the office?"

"I am, but my door's closed and I'm the first one here. What's up?"

"So, um, I realized that I need some guidelines around how to act around you at the office."

The woman behind him in line gave him a funny look, so he just waved her forward, too.

"I think that *we* need some guidelines about how we act around each other, and you're very wise to bring it up. Do you want to figure them out now?"

"Um, no, Daddy. I just wanted to know if I could bring you a coffee."

The woman in front of him turned around to stare. What the fuck was her problem? She was already in front of him, and it wasn't like he was even saying anything sexual. He was a firm believer that exhibitionism was only fun when everyone consented, but seriously? He was talking about coffee.

Nosey prude.

"That's very sweet of you, baby boy. Yes, you may."

"You like sugar, no milk, right?" He'd caught that order once on the phone and hung onto it ever since.

"That's right." Daddy seemed pleasantly surprised. "Thank you, baby."

"You're welcome, Daddy." He said the last word extra loudly. He wasn't going to let someone else's bullshit bring him down. Not when everything else in his life was perfect.

He waited till the nasty lady walked to the pick-up counter and ordered his three coffees.

When the barista called his name, there was a brown pastry bag with a folded top wedged between the three cups on the cardboard tray. Someone had written on it in marker, "Share it with your Daddy. XX"

He caught the barista's eye and made sure she saw him putting a ten in the tip jar while he called out his thanks.

After that, it was just a short trip to the office. His fingers were freezing from gripping his handlebars in the wind, but the coffees hadn't spilled in the milkcrate and bungee-cable set up he had going on. So he couldn't think of anything to complain about on such a glorious day.

When he got upstairs, he headed to his own desk first to drop off his coat. Then he left Christy's coffee in front of her keyboard. She wouldn't need a note to know who it was from. He lived near the good coffee shop and she lived near the good sandwich shop, so they had a system worked out.

Finally, he made it to Daddy's office, only to find Gabby from marketing lingering in the door. She was tossing one of those squishy stress balls into the air and catching it.

He looked at the stress ball the next time it came down. It was shaped like a butt plug, which must be a new design. He wondered who they convinced to manufacture them, and whether anyone would be stupid enough to try to actually use something with such porous material.

Probably.

Hopefully they had warnings on those things.

Gabby seemed to be deep in some recitation about her holiday plans.

Should he come back later? No, he decided. He and Daddy were hopefully going to spend years working together. That was the point of the HR changes and the contract. Better to start now.

"Hey Saul! Hey Gabby!"

Gabby greeted him, and he got close enough to see Saul waving him in. He surreptitiously looked down and made sure the writing on the paper packet was turned toward his chest.

"Gabby, sorry I didn't get you anything. I picked up some coffees on the way, but I didn't know who would be here."

"Sure," she teased. "I see you trying to get on the boss's good side."

Levi froze and he could see that Saul did, too. He knew it was a joke but, shit. It was a little too close to home.

Levi recovered first. "Yep. That three dollar coffee ought to be worth… what would you say, Saul? An extra one percent on my bonus?"

"At least," Saul agreed.

They all laughed and Gabby's butt plug ball bounced off the ceiling before she caught it. "No worries. I mostly drink tea anyway, and I'm taking off at noon. I only came in because I forgot the banner that I need for an event tomorrow. And I'm hoping that this box of magnets will come in. Actually, I should go check the mailroom. Bye, guys!"

As soon as she sauntered away, still tossing the obscene freebie, they both sighed. Levi shut the door.

"This is going to be harder than I thought," Levi admitted. He glanced at the couch and then quickly looked away. Forbidden office romances were hot in theory, but he was serious about maintaining his professionalism.

"Yeah, I was just thinking that." Saul rubbed his eyes.

"Is it too much? I mean, should we…"

"No, baby." Saul cut in quickly. "I mean, Levi. Er… Yeah. This is going to be difficult."

Levi set the tray of coffees down on the desk, waiting to take his cues from Da– Saul.

"Alright, let me try that again." Saul let out a deep breath. "Thank you, baby, for bringing me coffee. That was very sweet of you."

"You're welcome… Daddy. There was a mean lady who gave me the evil eye because she heard me talking to my Daddy on the phone, but then the barista gave me this!" He held up the packet. "I don't even know what's in it yet."

"Kinehora," Saul murmured with a smirk. It was the Yiddish word meant to avert the evil eye so that inexplicable curses wouldn't befall the recipient.

"Hey, I'm serious! She was giving me the evil eye, and I'm not going to let anything take my Daddy away."

"Well, in that case, why don't we sit down and talk about how things are going to work."

Levi scanned the couch again. It would be fun to sit there right now, just to torment them both, but their relationship was too important to risk. He took the chair that was closer to the desk. "So, what are you thinking?"

"First, that I need to talk to Javier as soon as possible. I thought he'd be in today, but he apparently won't be back till after New Years."

"Ugh."

"Well, it might be better to not have this all break while most of the staff is on vacation. I don't want it to look sneaky."

"Good point. But it's a long time to hide it."

"You're impatient, boy."

Levi nodded. Was he ever. He wanted *everyone* to know.

"Alright," he summarized. "So Javier comes back next Thursday or whatever. And then there will probably be lots of discussions and policy drafts and an official announcement that has been desiccated of any possible juicy details, so that'll be a few more weeks. Got it. What else?"

"Baby, did I ever tell you how much I admire that

you can switch so easily from being my adorable boy to a responsible colleague who can think things through with me?"

Levi felt himself blush. One of his exes had complained about exactly this—that he broke character sometimes, as if being Daddy's boy were some sort of play he was acting out. He knew he'd mentioned it, but he hadn't expected Saul to remember it.

"Thank you, Daddy. That means a lot to me."

"It means a lot to me, too. Whatever we decide, we should decide together. In the office we're equals. Or, you know, within the office hierarchy."

Levi nodded. He hadn't even considered any alternatives.

"So I was thinking that... for very short periods, with the door shut... we could talk to each other this way. But that's it. Just talk. No..." He gestured vaguely into the space between them.

"No dirty blowjobs under your desk while you're taking a call? Got it."

Saul laughed.

"And if we should find ourselves here together, debugging an error for six hours with nobody else around..."

"Then we are going to be responsible employees."

Levi wrinkled his nose.

"By which I mean that you will be an incorrigible flirt and I will make sure that you get a spanking when we get home."

Alright, Levi could live with that.

"I may also have to make sure that you're locked up so that you can be a good boy for me."

"Oooooh. Daddy, you have the best ideas."

"Well, if we're going to come into the office to work, I need to make sure that you're focused."

As if. But it was a fun idea. So, small flirty things were OK behind closed doors, but flirting was pretty much the limit. "What about around friends? Or if the staff goes out for drinks?"

"Then I think you can be my boyfriend, but with a respectful level of PDA. We won't be keeping it a secret. And if we see colleagues at a munch or play party, we'll treat it like we would with anyone else we know from outside."

Whew. That would have been even harder than managing things at work. Levi opened his mouth to ask his next question, but Saul beat him to it.

"Christy would be an exception, I believe."

"Yeah, um, if that's OK. She already knows about the spanking. And, uh, the only reason that she doesn't have all the details about the phone call yesterday was because I wanted to talk to you first."

"Good grief. And I have to stand in front of her at meetings?"

"If it helps, Chr… no, wait. Forget I said anything."

"Hang on, Christy and Nikhil?"

"Do you see it, too? It's mutual, right? But they haven't done anything. Promise. Though, uh, I did tell her that the HR policies might be changing."

"You are trouble, baby boy. And yes, I see it, too."

He pumped his fist in the air, then remembered he wasn't supposed to say anything. "Um, sorry."

"Don't apologize. You just want everyone to be happy, and you've thought about some realistic ways to do it."

"Christy helped."

"Of course she did." Saul shook his head. "Well, at least it'll be even. Could you leave at least a little delicacy around the details?"

"Just tell me what the limits are and I'll stick to them. I don't have to tell her anything if you don't feel comfortable with it."

"Maybe not until we all three… or maybe all four… sit down and talk about it. How about that?"

"Sounds good, Daddy. Um… I know this sounds strange, but I'm feeling much better now. I mean, I've already been having the best week of my life, but this just made it better."

"Really? Why?"

It took Levi a minute to put it into words. "I think that the past two days were kind of like… a fantasy. You know, where you dream it up, but you know it's not real. When we figure out the logistics, I feel like it means something. Like this isn't going away."

"No baby, it's not. I'm still figuring a lot of this out, but I'm your Daddy for as long as you want me." That was the third time Daddy had used the label, and he really shone.

Levi floated through the rest of the day.

He got a lot of work done, especially without all of

those pesky meetings, since most of the team was on vacation. He went out to lunch with Christy and enjoyed tormenting her with hints of details that he couldn't disclose.

He sent Saul a text at about 3:00 to see if he could stop by his office. He summarized the status on a new project, then got a kiss on the cheek and an invitation to spend the night. He drifted back to his cubicle, buzzing with delight.

This was better than any fantasy.

14

SAUL

Saul managed to leave the office by 6:30. Even while he was constantly wondering how Levi was doing and imagining what they could do together, he'd gotten a lot done today.

He'd always felt like Christmas week was prime productivity time for the Jews. Well, and everyone else in the office who was Hindu or Muslim or atheist. He'd only had one meeting today, and the office was nearly silent except for a few folks stopping by to say hello.

He'd heard Levi and Christy's laughter ring out over the cubicle walls once, and smiled fondly. It seemed like this was something that could really work.

Now he was going to swing by Levi's apartment, since he apparently didn't have a car and usually biked everywhere. It was very Portland of him.

Levi came down as soon as he texted, which was probably good because there was construction happening at the base of his building and the block was on the tram line. Even with his blinkers on, Saul had gotten honked at.

It was also good because it didn't give him time to wallow in his insecurities.

He hadn't quite been putting off spending the night together but… well, he kind of had. Levi might believe he was OK with dating a trans guy, but there was a lot of ground to cover between the idea and the reality.

Levi slipped into the car with a shout of "Daddy! I missed you!" and, well, it really was difficult to hold onto his anxieties in the face of such enthusiasm.

There was a car waiting behind him, so Saul eased back into the traffic. "You know we saw each other three hours ago, right?"

"I know. It was like forever." Levi sighed in classic Levi fashion.

Saul smiled as he turned onto the next street, just behind a bus. Even though this part of the city was on a grid, he'd be taking an unusual way home through the winding streets of Portland Heights, so he was depending on his GPS. It was probably nice for walking, but right now he was getting tangled up in one-way streets and rush hour.

When he finally glanced back at Levi, he was looking pensive.

"You OK, babe?"

"Is this too much?"

"What do you mean?"

"Just… you didn't seem excited to see me."

"Oh, babe." Saul put a hand out toward him, but

then had to grab it back to swerve in front of a car that stopped just in front of him. "Fuck!"

He finally stopped at a traffic light and gave him his full attention. "I have been thinking of nothing but you all day. I missed you, too. I'm just focusing on traffic because I want to get you back to my place and I need to keep you safe." He pressed his fingers to Levi's lips.

"So I'm not too much?"

"Nope. Never."

"Are you sure?"

Saul would never have guessed that Levi would need so much reassurance. He was so bright and excited so much of the time. At work, of course, he was completely responsible. He'd never struck Saul as someone who was innately insecure or unpredictable.

He just wished they could have this conversation somewhere else. "Babe, I am certain. Is there a reason you're worried so much about this?"

"I had an ex who thought I was over the top when I said things like that. I mean, at first he thought it was cute. But then I guess the honeymoon period was over. He got annoyed when I said I missed him after a few hours, and stuff like that. And you sounded kind of annoyed when you said it."

Saul reached over to find Levi's hand and brought it up to his lips for a kiss. "I meant it as a joke. I was annoyed that cars were honking at me. Never at you. And if I were ever annoyed with you, I would bring it up respectfully so we could discuss it."

"OK. And you really want me to come over tonight? It's not too many times? Do you, like, need a break?"

Saul kissed Levi's fingers again, then pressed Levi's hand to his own thigh so that he could make a turn. "I invited you, remember? Daddy doesn't need a break from his boy." He hoped Levi could hear how sincerely he meant it.

It was still a bit odd referring to himself in the third person, but it was really growing on him. "And I don't think I'll ever get tired of your enthusiasm. It's one of the things that I enjoy most about you."

"OK." Levi still sounded a bit wary.

"OK, what?"

"OK, Daddy." He could hear the smile returning to Levi's voice.

"Now tell me, darling boy. What would make tonight special for you?"

"Daddy," he replied promptly. Apparently that was the answer to the question.

"Thank you, sweetheart. But you need to be more specific." He had a few ideas, but he could be flexible. The central theme was just giving Levi what he needed.

"Just being with you, Daddy."

That still wasn't very helpful, but he was getting a feel for how his enthusiastic little monster liked to communicate. When he was being responsible, he was pretty direct and concise. But there was something about the Daddy/boy dynamic that made him a little squirrely about asking for what he wanted until he got too distracted or excited to realize he was saying it.

Since Levi wasn't innately shy, it was probably due to those assholes who he'd dated over the years. Saul wasn't going to let it rest, though. Levi just needed a little coaxing.

"Does being with Daddy mean that I make all the decisions?"

"Mmmm-hmmmm!"

"OK, I think we can arrange that. How about dinner and some cuddling?"

"Yes! And kisses?"

"Of course."

"And what if I'm naughty?"

Yeah, he knew Levi had plans for the evening. "Then I suppose you'd earn a punishment."

"Like spankings."

"Yes. And what if you were a good boy?"

"Oh, I would be a *very* good boy and get rewards." Saul didn't even need to glance at him to know he'd be bouncing with excitement.

"Definitely. Like what?"

"Tying me up and, well, doing whatever you want to do."

Bingo. Saul would definitely be setting some limits later, but for right now, all he wanted to do was spoil him. "So dinner, cuddles, and bondage?"

"And then more cuddles and you hold me while I sleep."

Saul could see how someone might interpret these delighted requests as pushy, but he liked that Levi asked for what he wanted. It meant that he didn't have to guess, and they could both get what they wanted. "That sounds like a perfect evening with my boy."

"Because you'll take care of me and I'm all yours."

Saul's heart melted. Sometimes Levi couldn't quite put his desires into words, but sometimes he said it so purely that it just cut right through him.

"That's right. Because I'll take care of you and you're all mine."

Inside the house, Levi spun in a small circle, looking at everything.

Saul tried to see it through his eyes. He'd bought the house when he'd been with his ex, and some of the furniture, like the black leather living room set, had been her choice. The art on the walls was all things that his friends had given him or he'd selected.

"I can't believe you have built-in bookshelves!"

Saul smiled. "I had those made when I got the house." He loved to read, and he found it comforting to bring his collection into the living room.

"And you have a fireplace! Does it work?"

"It does. I don't think I've used it in a year or two, but it should be OK. There's a woodpile in the back."

"Can we roast marshmallows?"

"Um… not sure I have those. And, uh, the vegan ones don't really melt."

"Kashrut doesn't apply to marshmallows. I mean,

are they really even made out of food? They're, like, sugar and clouds."

Clearly, Levi's kosher observance wasn't very strict. "Sugar, clouds, and cow hooves, but if you need marshmallows I'll get you marshmallows."

Levi snuggled up against him. Their height difference was immediately apparent, with Levi's armpit nearly level to his shoulder when he put an arm across his back. But when Levi was grinning about marshmallows, he didn't mind at all.

"Can we have a fire tonight?"

"If you don't mind putting your coat back on to get some wood."

"Sure!"

They made a quick trip out to the backyard just as the sun was setting. Levi grabbed a few logs, hefting them easily, while Saul shone his cell phone flashlight and held up the tarp.

"Just four is good. Any more than that and we won't be able to use them tonight, so we'd bring bugs into the house." Four was about all that Saul could usually carry, but for all that Levi was slender, it was clear that he could have grabbed twice as much. Longer arms. More muscle mass.

Saul just hoped that one day he'd stop worrying about things like that.

He grabbed a pile of kindling from the back porch on the way in, and snagged a few envelopes out of the recycling bin. With a judicious use of lighter fluid, he soon had a blaze going.

Levi settled beside him as they watched the flames. "Daddy, you're going to spoil me."

"I know, sweet boy. That's the plan."

"Yes, but you don't have to say yes to everything I ask for. Like, I think you didn't really want to go dancing yesterday. And we didn't need a fire."

"You know what? I didn't want to go, but then I had a wonderful time because I was there with you. And this fire place? I loved the detail when I bought the house, but I've only used it a handful of times. You make me appreciate things. Even more, though, it makes me happy to see you happy."

"I know. I just… I don't want to be greedy. I really meant it before that just being with you would be enough."

Saul turned so that they were both kneeling together. When he went up on his knees and Levi sat back on his heels they were the same height. But more importantly, it felt natural. Like they were finding the right ways to fit together.

He traced around Levi's face, getting to know the contours and dips, the first bristling edge of where his beard started. He was so precious.

"Don't ever be afraid of asking for what you want. I might not always give it to you. But that's just the thing, baby. I'm still new to this Daddy business, but I'm pretty sure that it's your job as my best bratty boy to ask for everything in the world. And it's my job as your Daddy to set reasonable limits when you need it and spoil you the rest of the time."

"Am I close to the limits?"

"For marshmallows and dancing? Nowhere close. I think you've missed out on a lot of spoiling that I need to make up for. If you want limits, though, I can think of plenty of other things."

"Like what?"

"Well, for one, I'd like to take control of your orgasms."

Levi shivered. "Yes, please, Daddy. I didn't even touch myself this morning in case you didn't want me to."

God, he was so perfect that Saul just had to kiss him. Slow and deep until Levi was melting into him. "Good boy," Saul whispered.

"For another, I think you like it when I order for you or when you need to ask me for permission for things."

Levi nodded eagerly. "Yes. That. But, um, only for little things. Is that OK?"

"That's what I was thinking. I don't want to run your life. I want to look after you."

"Whew. I had an ex and… well, he wanted to control my job and my money and my relationship with my family and just… It was horrible."

"Sweetheart, that sounds like abuse. If I ever do anything that makes you feel that way, I expect you to tell me right away. You can even safeword if you can't find another way to express it."

"Thank you. It was a long time ago and I feel like I

learned my lesson. Like, I know what to look out for. What do *you* want to control?"

"I want to learn everything that you love to eat so I can order it for you. I'd like you to check in with me each morning and night when we're not together. And if it's something you'd like, I'd love it if you asked me for permission to buy treats when I'm not with you."

"Like what?"

"I think that would depend on what you like. Desserts, maybe? Alcohol? Fun things that catch your eye?"

"And would you say yes?"

Saul gave him another kiss. "Probably almost every time."

"I knew you would be the perfect Daddy." Levi sighed happily and flopped down onto the floor. Saul leaned back against the base of an armchair and Levi wriggled around until his head was in his lap.

They sat that way for a while, watching the dancing flames. Well, Levi was watching the flames and Saul was watching the flickering glow on his skin.

"Daddy, what do you want?"

"At the risk of sounding unoriginal, I just want you."

"Uh-uh. You made me tell you all sorts of things, so now it's your turn. I want to make my Daddy happy."

"I think I'm a lot more boring than you. I work a lot, though I'll cut back to make more time for you. I like to read. I'm not very adventuresome."

"You say that, and yet you founded a kinky dating service."

Saul shrugged. "That's like the boring version of actually doing those things."

"But you have done them, right? I mean, the ones you're interested in?"

"Yeah. I trained with an experienced Dom and I've been in several kinky relationships, plus some more casual stuff at events and parties. I was kind of taking a break for a while, though."

"Why?"

Saul drew in a breath. He knew he had to have this conversation, so he might as well get it over with. At least here, in front of the fire with a snuggling boy in his lap was about as good a setting as he could ask for.

"I actually wasn't planning on getting involved with anyone until I was done transitioning," he finally admitted.

Levi gave him a funny look. "What does *done transitioning* mean? Like, is there an end point?"

"Maybe. In my head, I have this timeline. But I was mostly thinking that I wanted to feel more comfortable with myself. I was going to wait until I'd been on T for a couple of years."

"How long has it been?"

"A year."

Levi dragged Saul's hand up to his mouth and kissed it. "That's not important to me."

"I know you think that now, but… well, I don't know how much you know about trans guys. I may not be what you're looking for."

There. It was out.

Levi rolled his eyes. "Silly Daddy. You're my perfect Daddy, remember?"

"I just… Do you actually know what you're getting into? I mean, I heard you tell someone that you were completely gay."

"Oh, I'm definitely completely gay, which is kind of the point. I mean, OK, so I'm sure I don't know everything. But I have this friend, Quinn, who transitioned when I was in college. I went with him to get his first shot of T and took care of him when he got out of the hospital for top surgery. We never dated or anything, but, I mean, I talked through a lot of his concerns with him at the time."

"Not any more? Are you still friends?"

"He's kind of over it, I guess. Like, he's married with an awesome kid and the trans stuff doesn't seem to be as important in his life. But we're still friends. I've even told him about you."

"Because I'm trans?"

"Because I've had a crush on you for a year." Levi gave him a goofy grin.

Saul let a little bit of the tension leave his body. This conversation was going far better than he'd expected.

"Oh, and I've seen about a million before and after surgery pictures online," Levi piped up. "From when I was researching things with Quinn. Though I imagine surgical techniques have advanced since then."

"I haven't had any surgeries." Better to get that out there, too.

"I know." Levi still looked just as relaxed, just as happy and confident as he had before.

Though… that was awfully presumptuous. Saul flashed a look at him. Could he tell? Was it the way his chest looked? It was pretty flat already, and he always wore a binder, but maybe when he was wearing the t-shirt over the weekend instead of his usual blazer it had been more obvious.

"I mean, we met on the day you came out to the office, and you haven't had any two to three-week vacations since then. I suppose you could have had one earlier."

"Ah. Yeah. I just… OK. It sounds like you aren't new to this." Thank goodness. That was… a huge relief. "But I don't want to change your perceptions of me. Or disappoint you."

"The only way you could disappoint me is if you stopped acting like my Daddy." Levi gave him a look filled with such adoration that it was hard to doubt his honesty. "So, do you want to tell me about your body? Like, what terms to use or what's OK to touch and what's off-limits?"

Trust Levi to lead this conversation with absolutely no hesitation.

"Ha! I wish I knew. I kind of made peace with my body as, well, a butch lesbian. I mean, I didn't hate it. It's just that now that I'm letting myself identify as a man, I wish I could just be all the way there. I feel like a man, and I want all of my parts to match that. And… maybe this sounds silly, but being with another guy…

it's hard not to compare. So I don't… I just don't know yet."

When Levi responded, he was still upside down, but his voice was completely serious. It was fascinating watching him slip back into that mode. "I don't want to put any pressure on you to decide anything before you're ready. And I don't want to tell you how to feel about your own body. But from my perspective, you're a man, so all of your parts are man-parts. I won't be comparing. You just decide what you want to share with me."

Saul had to close his eyes just to take everything in. He'd been over this conversation so many times in his head with his hypothetical future partners. He'd expected to have to explain everything. To have to convince someone of his masculinity. To have to walk them through all the steps. Or maybe to avoid talking about it but wonder the whole time what the other person thought.

He knew that other trans guys didn't think it was a big deal. They went on hook-ups and blind dates, and clearly didn't have any problems. But he wasn't there yet.

So to have Levi, a gold star gay man, just tell him that he was *fine* with everything was such a relief that he wasn't even sure what to do next. It was like planning for a hurricane with all of his emergency essentials stocked up in his underground bunker, and then finding out it was just another sunny day.

Sunny days were good, but he wasn't sure what to do with all the leftover tension.

"I… Thank you," he finally managed.

"Nothing to thank me for. Oh, hang on. Funny story." Whatever Levi was thinking about, he'd already started to smile. It was one of the things that Saul loved about him—how honestly delighted he was with whatever was passing through his mind.

Saul quirked an eyebrow in inquiry. He needed a funny story right now.

"So remember that day of the interview? Well, I kept thinking, the whole time, my new boss is really sexy. We have such a great vibe together. And then I was like… OMG. Am I straight? Like, right in the middle of the interview I was thinking that. And, I mean, I haven't questioned my identity since I was, I dunno… six? But I was like… what if I don't know myself at all? Could I be straight? Then at the end you finally introduced yourself and I was like, *Thank God I'm still gay.*"

Saul burst out laughing. "Really? That's what you were thinking during that interview? *Thank God I'm still gay?*"

"Yeah. I mean, I was mostly thinking, *My new boss is so hot.* It was probably why I said all sorts of stupid stuff. I don't even remember most of what I said. You were just looking at me with your broody eyebrows, being all stern and Dominant. And then I would say something silly and you would smile, and you looked…

affectionate, I guess. And I was thinking, that's just how I want my Daddy to smile at me. But it was kind of confusing until you explained that you were a guy and I was like… Oh! Now it all makes sense. Phew. Still gay."

"That's seriously what you got out of that interview?"

"Well, yeah. New job working with Christy, some new friends to hang out with, and a hot Daddy to have office fantasies about. And I got to help pick your name. I still think that was pretty special."

"It was."

Saul wanted Levi closer. He dragged him up until Levi was nestled between his bent knees while they both watched the fire. It was finally starting to sink in that the conversation had gone alright, and all because of this bold, marvelous boy in his arms.

Levi turned his head for a kiss, and touching those soft lips felt like coming home. Like everything was right in his life.

Saul pulled back, but their breath still mingled. There were just no words for how special Levi was to him. How honored he was that he got to hold him like this. How awed he was that Levi was looking at him now with such trust and desire.

He watched some amusing thought pass Levi's face before he spoke. "One more thing."

"Hmmm?"

"I want to give you back massages. Pretty, pretty please? Without your shirt. That would be OK, right?"

Saul could only laugh as he squeezed him tighter.

The logistics of that sounded pretty manageable, even with his dysphoria. "Of course. I think I'm going to be a spoiled Daddy, too." Only Levi would think of that as a treat to beg for.

"Good." Levi rested his head on his shoulder. "That's how it should be. Because I have the best Daddy in the world."

15

SAUL

After sitting on the floor until Saul's back hurt and they were both starting to get hungry, they finally roused themselves for dinner. Saul checked in with Levi about food preferences again, because if he were going to be the "best Daddy in the world" as Levi put it, he wanted to know all of his boy's favorites.

So they'd looked at the menus from a dozen different restaurants, with both of them probably a little more turned on than they should be. It was intimate. A first little move toward their future together as Levi handed over pieces of his trust like gifts.

Of course, once Saul had privately decided what to order, he mentioned that there was leftover brisket and kugel from his mother's Hanukkah party in the fridge. Then Levi was batting his eyes at him, like he had to beg his way into what Saul would have given him anyway.

He could see how some of Levi's exes would have

found it over the top, but again, he loved all of that excitement. It was almost like Levi wanted to perform his role as a boy, just to make sure he knew exactly where he stood.

When Saul pointed out that the meal wasn't made in a Kosher home, Levi came up with some convoluted explanation that home-made food trumped kashrut. Especially if it looked Jewish. And pretty, pretty please, because it was homemade.

Saul realized that he was going to be making a lot of homemade meals.

So they shared a lazy dinner of microwaved leftovers and talked about building a fence around the Torah.

Which wasn't how he'd expected his evening to go.

The building the fence thing was the Jewish practice of, more-or-less, overcompensating and making up convoluted rules to carefully follow all of the religious decrees, especially when adapting them to a modern context. The first one he always thought of was that the Torah only said to not eat a calf in its mothers' milk, but just to be on the extra safe side, milk and meat couldn't even share the same air space in the oven or touch the same utensils.

Even if the meat was chicken, which obviously didn't have a milk-producing mother, in case there was an accidental mix-up. But eating the same chicken with the eggs it had literally laid the previous day, totally kosher.

Saul was actually pretty curious about Levi's explanation.

"I used to keep completely kosher. I didn't think about it. I grew up doing it, I ate at the kosher dining hall in the Hillel during college, and I learned to make exactly three meat dishes. I knew all the kosher brands, there are a few good restaurants, and I just… did it.

"But then, I started thinking about why I was doing it. Like, was it the actions or the intentions? Because I usually did it mindlessly. And, seriously, I met a lot of Jews in college who didn't keep kosher. So I finally talked to a Reconstructionist rabbi who didn't keep kosher, and she explained her practice of eating mindfully. She suggested I think about my values when I was buying food and cooking and eating. Like, was I choosing products that took care of the people producing them, the earth, and the animals that I was eating? Was I eating to delight in it instead of just rushing? Was I connecting to the parts of the Torah that felt meaningful to me?

"So for about two years, I didn't keep kosher at all. And let me tell you… bacon double cheese burgers are goooood."

Saul laughed. "I know."

"But after a while, I missed the routine. And I realized that it actually did make me more mindful about my eating. So now I follow something that's a bit more like eco-kashrut. Like, thinking of the values instead of just blindly following the dictates."

"So, would you eat milk mixed with meat if, say, it

was produced by a farm-to-table place where you knew everything had been made respectfully?"

Levi waved his hand side to side. "Maybe. I'd be more likely to order a meat dish without milk because I knew it had been raised and slaughtered humanely even though it wasn't done with all of the ritual supervision."

Saul was discovering that with every conversation they had, Levi fascinated him more. He didn't think they would ever get bored.

"So, were you really serious about studying Talmud?"

"Oh, completely serious. I mean, for me. That's not a requirement for a Daddy." He winked.

"Do you do weekly Torah study or something?"

"I'm doing Daf Yomi, actually."

"Sorry, I don't even know what that is. I mean, *yom* means *day*, right?"

"Yep. *Page of the day*. There's a seven-year cycle that takes everyone through the entire Talmud, which has, like, almost three thousand pages? You can subscribe to emails or podcasts where different rabbis discuss their interpretations of the ancient rabbis' interpretations for that day's page. We just started reading Pesachim, the laws about Passover."

"Which do you do? Email or podcast?"

"Podcasts when I have time. There are two that I like. And email when I get behind and just need to catch up. But I hit it about four or five days a week, and then use Shabbat to cycle back."

"So would you… like a chavruta?" That was a study partner, someone to carefully pore over a text with and then creatively argue about interpretations and applications.

Levi clapped his hands together. "No way. Daddy, really? I mean, really Daddy?"

"I'm probably going to regret this but… we could try it. You're going to know loads more than I do."

Levi shook his head. "That doesn't matter. We can do all of it in English. One of my podcasts is English only, and there's definitely a good email that one of my friends gets. I'll have to ask her which one it is."

"So you listen in Hebrew?"

"No, not fully. The discussion is in English, but when they quote the text and references it's in Hebrew."

Yeah, Saul was going to be way out of his depth. But he could see how important it was to Levi. And honestly, he figured that talking about Talmud with someone so clearly passionate about it was going to be a very different experience than his death-by-boredom Hebrew school lessons as a kid. It would be a different kind of doing something special together.

"So, tell me about Pesachim."

"Well, in the most recent one I read, 14a, I think, the rabbis were arguing about whether meat and oil that were made ritually impure by touching someone who had touched something impure could still be used in sacrifices at the same time."

Phew. Right. Talmud. People were still studying this

hundreds of years later, even though temple sacrifices hadn't been made in two thousand years. "So what did they conclude?"

"They didn't. Or at least not that I've read so far. I believe the oil can contaminate the oil, but the meat works differently. At any rate, what I take from it is actually pretty much what I was saying before. That you should be thoughtful when you eat. Or at least when you make sacrifices. Like, the details are important and everything is connected."

Huh. That was a lot to think about. "What does this have to do with Pesach?"

"Oh, it all kicks off with something weird about watching oxen to see how long they can plow to know when to start cleaning the chametz"–that was the raised bread that people ate during the rest of the year–"out of the house to get ready for Passover. Then they're like… speaking of oxen, remember this unrelated thing about meat? OK, go."

Saul chuckled. Fine, so Daf Yomi was probably going to be intense, but Levi would at least make it fun. And probably surprisingly insightful.

"I think I could commit to… maybe once a week? On Shabbat, maybe?"

Levi bounced out of his chair to cover his face with kisses.

He was just so… joyful. So amazingly easy to delight. Saul could already imagine days and weeks and years of this exhilaration in his life.

While Levi was already close, Saul pulled him down

onto his lap. "So… speaking of Passover… Were you serious about having me meet your family, too?"

Levi shone and the sloppy, enthusiastic kisses began all over again. "First night with my family and second night with yours?"

"My mother would love that, if you're willing to drive up to Seattle." Maybe it was too soon to say such things. God, it sounded so domestic. Like they were married already or something.

But they'd known each other for most of a year, and, well, Saul had a pretty good feeling that they'd still be going strong come spring. Everything that Saul found out about Levi as a sub and a boyfriend, if that's what they were, and, well, a Talmud scholar, just made it better.

They eventually settled back down to eating dinner, giving each other silly grins across the table. It was just… he'd never taken anyone home for Passover. Well, college friends, of course. But never someone he was dating. Some of them hadn't lasted long enough and some of them hadn't been Jewish.

His mother would be thrilled to meet Levi.

Another thought occurred to him. "Levi, what does *neshama* mean?" He pronounced it like most Hebrew words, with the accent at the end.

"Hmm? Oh, it means soul or spirit or breath. Like you've probably heard *Kol haneshama tehallel Yah* is let everything that has breath praise the Holy One."

"That sounds vaguely familiar. And how about

motek?" He made the first syllable soft and gentle, more like *mah*, with the accent on the second.

"Awww… are you thinking about nicknames for me?"

"Um, yeah. My grandfather called my grandmother those names. But I didn't know what they meant. Like, it could have been something weird or derogatory, too."

"No, those are both adorable. *Matok* means sweet, and *motek* is a variation that's like sweetheart or honey or sweetie. And *neshama sheli* would be my soul. Of course, in English it sounds really dramatic and poetic to call someone 'my soul.' In Israel people kind of toss it around casually. Like, you could call your neighbor's kid that or say it in your wedding."

"So it's still special?"

"It would be very special." Levi promised. He propped his head on his folded hand and just looked up at Saul adoringly. It was a little bit posed and very Levi.

"I was also thinking about *simcha.*" He mangled throat-clearing sound on the *ch*, but he felt like he got it close enough. "That means joy, right? And people use it as a name?"

"I'm your simcha?" Levi practically fluttered out of his chair.

"Apparently." God, Saul's cheeks were going to hurt from smiling so much. He was sure he looked just as dopey as Levi did.

"So," Levi asked eagerly, "does that mean that you're

my *abbale*?" The word was soft and rolling in his mouth, *AH-buh-luh*, like a verbal cuddle.

Levi was looking it him like he was suppose to know what it meant. "Your... oh, like *abba* means father?"

"Mmmm-hmmmm..." Levi left it for him to figure out the rest.

The ending sounded kind of cute. Oh. *Oh.* "So that means daddy?"

"My abbale. If that's OK with you."

Saul held open his arms for Levi to launch into them again. "Come here, baby. My... motek." He couldn't even remember the *my* part in Hebrew, but it didn't matter. That was Levi. His sweetheart. His joy. Maybe even his soul.

They were cleaning up a few dinner dishes when Saul pulled Levi to him. He was still so much taller, but he turned easily into Saul's arms, always ready to be guided.

"So, we've had dinner and cuddles. I believe I promised you one more thing tonight."

Saul could see the moment when Levi figured it out. "Oh, yes, please, Daddy! I'm ready."

"Don't you even want to know what we're doing?"

Levi shook his head. "I already know. My Abbale's going to take care of me."

"You're right." He pulled Levi down for a kiss. He'd

still talk through everything he wanted to do, but he could ask permission as he went along. "My bedroom's the first room at the top of the stairs. There's a bathroom inside if you'd like to use it. I'll be up in a little bit, and I want to find you naked."

"Yes, Daddy!" Levi raced for the stairs, came back to give him another kiss, and finally left the room. Adorable.

Saul finished putting away the food and closed up the fireplace. When he heard the footsteps above him cease, he headed up and paused in the doorway.

Fuck. Levi was breathtaking. He'd decided to kneel, his lean muscles and sparse hair all on display. His head was bent, those soft curls hiding part of his face and exposing his elegant neck. His dick was hard and leaking, such a visible symbol of his arousal.

Saul was met with both envy and desire. It was endlessly disappointing knowing that his body wouldn't look or work like that without several surgeries that he might not decide to get.

On the other hand, Levi's cock was all his now to play with and explore. It was even more heady knowing that he was giving himself over to Saul's control.

Hopefully he could get this right. He hadn't just made Levi touch himself last night because it was sexy as hell. He'd also been watching very closely for instructional purposes.

Instructional purposes that had him jerking off

when he got home, naturally. His boy had been magnificent.

He walked a little closer and Levi looked up with a goofy grin, destroying the facade of trained submission. Now he didn't look submissive so much as playful. Levi had definitely followed his commands with alacrity yesterday, but the more formal D/s stuff didn't seem to fit him. Which was probably why he was looking for a Daddy as much as a Dom.

Saul walked around him, amused as Levi turned his head to follow him with his eyes and then whipped his neck around when he couldn't twist any further. God, he'd be horrible at high protocol. Fortunately, Saul didn't need that. Levi's enthusiasm more than made up for it.

With some other subs, he might try to be more formal himself, more distant and removed to heighten his dominance. But it didn't seem right with his boy. It felt more like they were building something together.

Levi so fervently gave up control that all Saul had to do was put out his hand and accept it. And in return, he was so obviously already Levi's Daddy so he didn't need to prove it. He just needed to take care of him.

Saul ran his fingers through Levi's hair. "How are you doing, babe?"

"Good. Really good."

"You asked for bondage tonight. Is that still what you want?"

Levi looked up at him with half-lidded eyes. It was

like he was already floating just from the idea of it. "Yes, please."

"I'd like to bind you completely. No movement at all."

Levi shivered, nodding against Saul's hand.

"I'd like to blindfold you, too. When I know you better, I'd like to play with some other sensory deprivation, but right now I want us to be able to hear each other."

"Thank you, Daddy."

"I'd like to use my crop on you. Mark your gorgeous skin."

This time Levi moaned.

"Any health concerns I should know about?"

"Nope."

"What are your safe words?"

"Red and yellow."

"Good boy. We're still learning each other, so just talk with me. Let me hear you, but also let me know what you like. Alright?" Not that Levi had shown any hesitation in voicing his opinions in the past.

"Yes, Daddy."

"I'm going to get a few things set up. Why don't you come over and watch?"

Levi grinned up at him and scrambled off the floor to hover next to him.

Saul was glad that he'd guessed correctly. Levi wanted the mystery, but even more, he wanted to be involved and he wanted to stay close.

Saul grabbed the pile of nylon and velcro straps from

a box in his closet and started laying them out horizontally on the bed, spaced about six or eight inches apart.

"Ooh! Are those for me, Daddy?"

Obviously, but Saul didn't say that. Whether Levi was seeking affirmation or was just excited, his feelings were more important than any logic. "Just for my boy."

"I can do these ones."

"Go ahead. Put the shorter ones at that end." The longer straps, intended for Levi's torso, were around five feet long, but there was a set for his legs that were closer to two feet.

Saul would have thought that having Levi help would take away some of the awe and thrill, but Levi looked almost reverent as he placed the straps. He ran his fingertip down the soft velcro of the last one, like it was something to remember and treasure.

"Lay down when you're ready. On your back."

Levi climbed gingerly onto the bed. Some of the straps shifted and pooled together but they could be fixed later. When he settled into the middle, he looked up at Saul beatifically.

"Color?"

"Soooo green."

Saul knelt on the bed and wrapped the first strap around Levi's shoulders, just above his nipples. He settled the next one just below.

The next three followed easily. Belly. Hips. Thighs.

That was when Levi started to squirm. The last strap both trapped his wrists, leaving his arms completely immobile, and gave a hint what was coming for his legs. It also landed just below his exposed cock. But was he squirming because he was uncomfortable or just to test the limits of the bonds?

"How are you doing, baby? Anything too tight?"

"No, Daddy. It's perfect. More, please." That sounded like Levi. Squirming just to see if he could. Just to know that he couldn't move.

Saul secured the final three. Just above the knee, just below, and ankles. There was one strap that he hadn't used and he was about to toss it aside, but he realized it could serve a better purpose. Lifting Levi's feet, he tucked it into the ankle strap and then secured it to the bar at the foot of the bed.

Now Levi was truly immobilized. And gorgeous. So fucking gorgeous Saul could scarcely breathe. The pattern of creamy skin and dark bands was exquisite, showcasing Levi's lanky limbs and slender chest. Of course, the centerpiece was his cock, so full and hard that it stood an inch above his belly.

But it was the willing submission that hit Saul the hardest. The knowledge that this man, this playful, beautiful, confident, hurt man, was trusting all of himself to him. There was nothing that could match the erotic thrill and deep sense of protectiveness that Saul got seeing him this way.

Levi wiggled again, then let out a deep sigh of contentment.

Saul came up and gave him a lingering kiss. Levi

melted beneath him, letting Saul set the pace while he tangled their tongues together and nibbled at his lips.

"How do you feel, baby?"

"Mmmmm… cozy and sexy."

Saul chuckled. That was what he'd been going for, but Levi just sounded so smugly pleased about it. Bondage was usually such a serious affair, at least in Saul's experience. Levi made it silly and fun.

"Ready for the blindfold?"

"Yes, please."

Saul kissed each of his eyelids, then fit the sleep mask around his head. Levi turned his head both ways, as though checking that everything was still there around him. Adorable.

There were two purposes for the mask. One, of course, was to heighten every one of Levi's sensations, to make every touch unexpected and sensuous.

The other one was more personal for Saul and he'd planned it out in advance. He wanted time to explore Levi's body—a cis male body—without having to hide his own reactions or wondering what Levi was thinking of his own less than ideal body.

Now that Levi couldn't watch him, he shucked off his slacks and collared shirt and tossed them on the chair. He had no plans to get completely naked, but in his undershirt and boxers he'd be able to feel much more of Levi's skin if he wanted to.

So the blindfold was a bit of security, a way for Saul to keep his own confidence so that he could give Levi all of his attention.

"Daddy? What are you doing?" Levi didn't sound worried, more curious.

"I'm taking off my clothes."

Levi pouted. "And I don't get to see?"

Saul bent over and gave him a kiss. "I thought you liked mysteries."

"No, I like treats."

Saul kissed him again. It was nice to know that Levi thought of his body as a treat, even if he wasn't quite ready to share it. "Don't worry. I have plenty of treats for you."

Levi beamed.

Truly, Levi was the treat. Just seeing him bound on his bed made something pulse hot and carnal inside of him.

He was going to start slowly, though. Enjoy every moment of discovering his boy and dragging screams of pleasure from him.

Levi's body was lightly covered with coiled hair and Saul dragged his hands over it, just far enough from the skin to feel Levi's warmth without ever touching him. He'd never dated anyone with so much body hair, and he loved seeing how it accentuated Levi's slender muscles.

Levi whimpered and hummed.

Saul had always been attracted to both men and women, but the automatic assumptions that men seemed to make about him had turned him off. When he'd dated women, he had been, by comparison, the masculine one. Not just the Dom, but, if he were being honest with himself, the man in the relationship.

Now that he'd finally admitted to himself who he was and taken the steps to achieve it, he could be the man *and* be with another man.

Not to mention that taking T had turned his sex drive up to a thousand. It had also led to him increasingly thinking about flat chests and hard cocks rubbing together when he fantasized.

Everything with Levi, though, was so much more.

He let his hand drift down, still hovering over Levi's skin, across his belly and then over each thigh. He circled around again, getting closer to his target, but still avoiding Levi's cock. A little pool of precum dripped onto his belly.

Saul would probably never have that for himself, on his own body. But for right now, Levi's cock was his, too.

He floated his hand over Levi's balls, which were already full and tight. Levi trembled beneath him.

"Did you touch yourself, baby? While you were waiting for me?"

"Only a liiiiiiittle bit."

Saul grabbed the hairs beneath his fingers and gave them a tug. Not hard enough to really hurt the delicate sac, he hoped, but enough to make a point.

"Daddy!" Levi yelped. His erection didn't abate at all. "Oh, fuck, Daddy." Awed pleasure filled his voice.

Definitely a little pain slut. But then, Saul had known that already from their conversation about limits earlier. "If you think you can take care of your-self..." he teased.

"Oh, no, Daddy. Only you. It's yours."

"That's what I thought." Then he moved his hands back up to Levi's chest, gliding over the fuzzy hair on his pecs.

"Daddy! Aren't you going to touch me?"

"I thought you said that your gorgeous cock was mine. Don't I get to decide?"

Levi scrunched his nose and Saul had to bite back a laugh. "You're torturing me," he grumbled.

"That's what happens to naughty, sexy boys who play with themselves without permission."

Levi squirmed in his bonds again. He wasn't going to get very far that way, but Saul figured he was welcome to try.

Now that he'd made his point, he bent to finally feast on Levi's skin the way he'd been wanting to for so long. He started with Levi's neck, licking the thick cords as Levi twisted back to give him access.

He drifted down to Levi's shoulders and chest, enjoying the captured strength of his lean muscles. The springy hair got in his mouth, so he licked and mouthed harder to taste the flesh below it.

He encountered the first strap and licked a line just above it, making sure Levi remembered that it was there.

Levi's breath was rapid. It was intoxicating knowing how turned on he was from just a little teasing, barely the beginnings of their explorations together.

Finally, Saul skipped over the strap and made large circles around Levi's nipples. He followed the same paths with his tongue and one hand, exploring the textures and tastes that made up his boy.

He reached the first bud and got a moan in reward. They were small, flat nubs, hardly anything to wrap his lips around, but he sucked and fondled until Levi was panting.

"Are these still sore, boy?" He kept his mouth wet and heavy over it while he spoke.

Levi nodded, then shook his head.

"Try again, boy."

"Just a little bit. Not much."

"Hmmm… let's fix that, shall we?"

"Ye… Daddy!" Levi shrieked as Saul bit and twisted at the same time. His back arched up from the bed. "Daddy! Oh, God. Daddy, that's…ohhhhh…"

Saul licked soothingly around them. "You like that, don't you."

"Mmmmm…"

"Let's figure out what else you like." Saul drifted further down, sucking and biting along Levi's belly. He loved how the hair got thicker below Levi's belly button, a little pathway to follow.

A pool of precum was tangled in Levi's curls and he darted in to lick it. It was… bitter. Like… well, he wasn't sure what it was like. Nothing he'd ever tasted before.

He swallowed, then tried to dissect the odd aftertaste.

The thing it reminded him of most was the remnants of thick grape juice at the bottom of a kiddush cup. He couldn't figure out why it would taste like that at all. Maybe some interaction with the acidic juice and the metal. What an odd connection. Of course, it wasn't exactly the same, but there was something similar.

He would have to remember to tell Levi that later. He'd certainly get a kick out of it, but right now Saul didn't want to break the sensual mood he was building.

This was exactly why he'd wanted the blindfold. Levi didn't need to see him making funny faces at his first taste of semen in the middle of a scene.

He drifted down further, nibbling at the jutting bones of Levi's hips and then tracing down his legs. Levi's thighs were lean, but his calves were thick with bitable muscle. All of that biking apparently had an effect.

Levi's muscles were trembling as he touched them.

He mouthed down to Levi's feet, amused when Levi tried to yank away from him and was brought up sharply by the strap that anchored him to the bar.

"Ticklish?"

"Yeah. It, um, actually makes me feel queasy."

Better not to do that, then. Saul kissed his way back up, making a wandering path that crossed over the straps and then back again.

He stopped just before he reached Levi's erection,

smoothing both hands across the skin surrounding it. Levi drew in a sharp breath.

It seemed larger up close. So hard and forceful, but also exposed and vulnerable, especially framed by those constricting black straps.

Slowly he moved one hand up over Levi's balls and then around the shaft. He hadn't expected it to be so warm. And the skin was… there was just no word for it.

Impossibly silky and tender. Loose enough to glide over the hardness beneath in a way that just begged to be played with. Saul tightened his grip and gave a few exploratory strokes. It felt magnificent in his hand, long and thick like it was supposed to be.

"Mmmmmm… Daddy. Like that, Daddy."

He loved how vocal Levi was about what he wanted. Not that he was always going to give it to him, but at least he'd never wonder if he was doing it right.

He raised his other hand to the exposed crown, palming it in a circle the way Levi had demonstrated last night.

"Oh, yeah. Like *that*, Daddy." Levi panted.

Saul wanted to taste it. If it was that soft in his hand, he could only imagine how satiny smooth it would feel against his tongue.

He put his lips around the head. Oh, yes. It was even better than he'd expected.

He played with the round knob, investigating the sounds he could make. Circles with his tongue made Levi whimper. Strong sucking made him moan. The hint of teeth made him gasp and shake. And burrowing into the slit made him cry out and struggle.

Saul was definitely going to be doing a lot more of this.

There was one more thing he wanted to try. He rubbed his thumb over the frenulum, accompanied by Levi's rising moans.

Then, still stroking with his other hand, he pinched it and didn't let go.

Levi's whole body went stiff, even his breath stopped. Then he started gulping in lungfuls of air, his hips jerking around.

When Saul finally went back to a soothing caress, Levi was still breathing hard. And his erection was still firm.

"Color?"

"Ugh. Green. Fuck!"

"Did you like that?"

"Shit. Yes." Levi sucked in another breath. "But don't expect me to ask for it." The nose scrunch was back.

"Tell me more."

"It's just… it's good because you're doing it. But it turns me all tight inside and it hurts and I feel all jangly everywhere and… ugh. I don't even know why I like it so much."

"Because you're a little masochist, sweetheart. And you need Daddy to give you the right amount of pain." Fuck was it a rush saying that sentence. Each time he called himself Daddy, he could feel himself embracing the role more.

"Yes, Daddy. Please." Levi begged so sweetly.

"Are you ready for more?"

"That, again?"

"I was thinking of the crop."

"Yes. I mean… maybe not on my dick?"

"Definitely not until I know your body much better. Especially when I can get such a reaction from just doing this." He flicked the shaft sharply.

Levi moaned. It looked like that was just the right amount of pain. Anything else they'd have to work up to or maybe not even play with.

He gave it another flick, lower down. Oh, yeah. Levi *really* liked that.

"Don't come," Saul warned before dragging the tip back into his mouth while he flicked the base again and again, always in a different place.

"Daddy, Daddy, Daddydaddydaddydaddy gonna come!"

Saul drew back, his own breathing hard. Fuck, Levi was gorgeous like that, all breathless and desperate and just on the edge of his release.

"Daaaaaaaaaaaddyyyyyyyyy."

It was amazing how many ways that word could come out of his boy's mouth. He ignored the complaint, of course. Because every single box that had to do with edging, denial, and orgasm control had been checked a vivid green on Levi's list. Because it was the first thing he'd mentioned when he described what he enjoyed.

Instead, Saul leaned across the bed to pick up the

crop.

Since Levi couldn't see, he flicked it across his own arm. It only took the slightest twist of the wrist to elicit a sharp sting, something Saul always tested on himself before playing.

At the sound, Levi's head darted toward him and his lips parted in desire.

Saul trailed the crop over Levi's chest and down his legs. This was all about building up the anticipation.

He roved back up to Levi's thigh, the safest part of the body to hit, and just held it in one place. And held it. And held it.

Levi was perfectly still, barely breathing.

And then he pulled back and slapped it back in the same place. A red splotch bloomed on his skin.

"Ow!"

Saul chuckled. Levi sounded like he was complaining, but he was still as hard as a rock. Penises were quite useful that way.

Saul tapped more gently the next time, setting up a slow rhythm of little butterfly flicks across Levi's thighs until the endorphins started flowing.

Levi's body was tight at first, his fingers clenched. Then he started slowly to relax, moaning softly while his hands hung down within the straps.

When he moved to the next phase, grunting and trying to fruitlessly pump up into the air, Saul increased the pressure.

"Ohhhh…"

That was it. The same sharp strike that had been so unpleasant before was now sending Levi soaring.

Saul shifted focus to Levi's chest, starting again with the gentle warming flicks and alternating occasionally with harder strikes against Levi's thighs.

When he was moaning just as much from both sensations, Saul increased the pressure of each strike. It still didn't take much of his own effort to leave bright, searing marks on Levi's pale skin and having him groaning and arching into each swing as it came.

Saul didn't follow any pattern, alternating between the two sites to keep Levi alert with anticipation.

He thwacked down on one nipple and Levi just begged for another. Back to his thighs. Low on the right, high on the left. Then the other nipple.

Levi was shaking and moaning, crying out for more though all of his skin was a fiery red. Saul probably could have continued a little longer, but he wanted to end while Levi was still on a high.

He tossed the crop on the bed and ran soothing hands over both areas, working the sting into the muscles beneath.

"You took those so good for me, baby. You're all red from my marks."

Levi nodded, his neck loose and head tilted back. "Good for Daddy."

"That's right, sweetheart. So good for me."

Next time he wanted to take a picture of that bright red skin against the solid black straps. To show Levi how gorgeous he was. Photos and videos had been a big yes for Levi, but Saul couldn't bear to leave him for even an instant to get his phone.

When he felt like Levi had had enough soothing, Saul shifted around to straddle his straight, bound legs. Now it was time for his good boy to come.

He imagined it wouldn't take much.

He kissed the tip of his straining erection, pausing just long enough to make sure Levi was with him and still wanted it.

"Oh, Daddy!"

Without any further preliminaries, he pulled Levi's cock into his mouth, taking as much as he could. He overestimated, though, and fought back a gagging response. How did people even do that? Alright, blowjob skills: something he'd need to practice.

But he liked holding it in his mouth, feeling the warmth and girth. Feeling how, with each tiny lick, Levi twisted his hips upward for more. Feeling powerful as he held that delicate, sensitive part of Levi next to his sharp teeth, so that he could control exactly how he wanted to give Levi everything he needed.

His boy was straining against his confinement, pumping upward though he could barely move an inch. He clearly loved being so tightly bound. Even with the mask, Saul could see his forehead wrinkled as his eyes closed tightly. His mouth was open and desperate.

Saul jerked him with one hand and cupped his balls with the other, never removing his mouth from the tip.

"Daddy? Can I come? CanIcomeDaddypleaseplease-please, pleeeease?"

"Come, baby," he breathed over his cock, before sucking him down hard.

That was all it took and Levi was screaming out his orgasm, thrashing against his bonds and arching into Saul's body.

Saul's mouth filled with the bitter fluid. He thought about swallowing, but he didn't have anything to prove. He spit it back into his hand, letting it trail down Levi's cock. It was white and foamy when he spread it around in the last final jerks as Levi shuddered through the aftershocks.

"Daddy, want you."

He'd been expecting that. Saul was still so hard he was nearly dying from it, but he was going to hold his baby now while he came down.

"Want you to come, too. Please."

Now that he hadn't been expecting.

"Please. Want to make you feel good. Come all over me. And I can't see anything. Please, Daddy." The words were all strung together, just as needy and desperate as what he'd asked for before.

Saul considered it. Levi was right. He *couldn't* see him. Behind that blindfold, it would be just sound, touch, and their own imaginations.

His filthy, perfect boy. Not just selfless, but affirming. And so fucking hot the way he begged. "You want me to jerk off all over you?"

"Please."

"Because you haven't had enough?" Saul thrust his

clean hand into his briefs, behind his packer. He could do this.

"Not enough. Want you."

Saul's other hand was still on Levi's cock, the veins still pulsing under his fingers.

He stroked his own smaller dick hard. Fuck was it good. He loved the idea of coming all over Levi. A dirty fantasy that they could both enjoy together, even if the logistics didn't quite match. "I'm touching my cock, baby. Just like I'm touching yours."

Saul started up the same rapid pace around Levi's shaft, cum and saliva making it shiny and smooth. Levi groaned, enjoying the additional sensation, then seemed to realize what was happening.

"Daddy, no! Too much!" His face was screwed up in misery from the overstimulation.

Saul didn't let up. This was something Levi had asked for, too. He gripped a little tighter.

"Oh, god, Daddy. I can't!" Levi tried to sit up, but it was impossible with the bindings and Saul heavy on his thighs. He fell back against the bed.

"Yes you can, baby. You're going to come for me and I'm going to come all over you."

"Daddy, daddy, can't! Too much!"

Saul circled the head with his palm, making the same motion on himself. Fuck. Fuck, he was so close. Watching Levi thrash and try to twist away only made it better.

"You want to be a good boy for Daddy, don't you?"

"Yes! Please, Daddy."

"That's right. You make me so hard, getting to see you like this. Watching you take it for me."

"Yes, Daddy." Levi was starting to arch up into his hand again, pressing himself into the discomfort in his need to obey.

Saul could feel his own orgasm rising. His heavy moans mingled with Levi's.

"Oh, God. Oh please. Just like that. Just like…. Daddyyyyyyyyy!"

Nothing was slowing him down now. Levi was screaming underneath him as cum shot from his dick.

Saul tumbled over the edge, molten pleasure washing through him. He was drowning in it, swept away by sensation and Levi's glorious scream as they melded together into one.

The second he finished, he tore through the velcro crossing Levi's chest. One, two, three, four harsh sounds and then Levi's arms were free. Saul dove toward his chest, yanking off the blindfold.

He needed to see Levi, needed Levi to see *him*. Needed to be so close they never came apart.

He covered Levi's mouth with hungry, open kisses. They devoured each other, Levi's arms coming up around him to hold tight.

Fuck. This wondrous, beautiful boy, who had been so open and needy in his submission. Who had taken everything Saul had to give him and reveled in it. Who had begged for his *Daddy* to come and actually made Saul feel safe enough to do it.

At last, their kisses slowed, becoming tangled and sweet like honey.

Saul pulled back but Levi wouldn't let him go.

"I just need to free your legs, sweet boy. My *motek*." His sweetheart. "Then I'll be back."

Levi sighed, but didn't attempt to disagree with the choice. Even with the soft mattress beneath him, he'd been in that position for a long time.

Saul removed all the straps, then worked his way up, rubbing each line that was pressed into Levi's skin and helping him to move his joints.

Levi lay back, hips and knees bent, dick floppy and soft between them.

Saul snuggled into Levi's open arms, wrapping their limbs together.

With someone else, he might have worried about being the smaller, lighter one, the one who was being held instead of holding. But with Levi, he just wanted to be close.

They drifted for a while that way, soaking into each others' bodies. Saul could never get enough of the scent of Levi's sweat, warm from their exertions.

He only moved when Levi started to shift a little, like he was getting uncomfortable. Saul rolled them both to their sides and rested his head on Levi's shoulder.

"How was that, my simcha?" he asked against Levi's skin, testing out the word. His joy.

"Perfect, Abbale." He could hear the happiness in Levi's voice just from saying the word.

"Mmmm… It was pretty perfect for me, too. Any other feedback?" It might not be as sexy as just guessing, but checking in after scenes was important.

"Oh, you know. Just that it was probably the best scene in my whole life."

Saul looked up. "Really?"

"I mean, last night was spectacular, too."

"I wasn't fishing for compliments." Though he couldn't deny he loved hearing them. He wanted so much to know that he was making Levi happy.

"I know, Daddy. I'm just being honest. It was just… well, technically you didn't do anything that no one else has ever done. But it was the way that you put them all together. It was like I was flying and never had to come down.

"But more than that," he continued, "it felt different because you're my Daddy. Because you care about me. Right?" His voice got a little smaller at the end.

For all his hesitation, Levi was always the bold one. Always one step ahead.

It had only been two days. Well, two days and most of a year of pining. Wasn't it too soon?

On the other hand, how could he call Levi his boy if he couldn't admit that he cared about him? Especially when he was looking so hopeful, and when he'd been hurt so badly in the past.

Especially when it was true. "I do care about you. So much more than I probably should right now. But I do."

"Perfect."

16

LEVI

I t was Christmas.

Christmas was weird.

Levi biked through the mostly empty streets. For once, the sun was shining. The air was warm and crisp.

Everything was closed.

A few cars passed by, but nothing like the normal traffic for this time of day. A family walked down the street, chattering, but it didn't compare to the typical foot traffic.

It was always a Twilight Zone experience walking around on Christmas. Like he'd been ported to some other dimension where ninety percent of the population had been removed and the rest were part of some giant conspiracy.

Obviously, he understood that it was a special family holiday for most people, but it was still strange being an outsider to the largest national holiday of the year. It wasn't that he wanted to be part of it—the Jews had holidays practically once a month plus Shabbat every week, so he wasn't struggling on that front.

It was just strange observing the bulk of American culture perform a ritual—largely for marketing purposes as far as he could tell—for about six weeks every year that he wasn't a part of. It made him feel a little out of sync with the rest of the country. Though it wasn't as strange as trying to explain Jewish holidays to people.

He turned the corner and discovered that the Bangladeshi grocery store was open. Awesome. Maybe he could stop there and get some drinks and snacks on the way back.

He biked the rest of the way to his favorite Chinese restaurant, one of the few that had a full selection of tasty vegan meat substitutes. He leaned his bike outside. Usually he'd lock it, but there was no one on the sidewalk and the owner was always quick to bring out his order.

They chatted for a few minutes, mostly about how surprisingly sunny it was, and then he was back on his bike, the food nestled in the milk crate over his back tire.

He had a similar chat with the owner of the Bangladeshi grocery store where he picked up some mango juice, a quart of olives from the barrel, and some homemade sweets. He got rasmalai, the soaked cheese balls in the milky cardamom juice, and something new he couldn't remember the name of, though it looked pretty.

Halfway home, he realized that he was supposed to have texted Saul before buying the sweets.

Instead of feeling guilty or naughty, he felt joyfully light. He had a Daddy now to ask permission from.

He locked his bike up in the basement and brought everything upstairs.

The first thing he did was take out the two desserts, make sure the lighting was good, and take a picture.

Levi: Hey Abbale.

He had to teach his phone the new word, since he figured he'd be using it a lot. That Saul had thought about giving him a Hebrew nickname was endlessly touching. And using the nicknames in most places would feel a little bit like a secret world they were part of. Among Jews, they'd feel like an old married couple or something.

There was nothing he didn't love about it.

He still needed to send the picture, of course.

Levi: I got these for us but I forgot to ask.

He added a blushing emoji to the end and sent it.

A moment later he got an answering chime.

Daddy: Thank you for telling me, baby boy. We'll see if you're good enough to earn them later.

Daddy: Be there in about twenty minutes, my simcha. Just heading out the door.

Levi sent back a heart emoji and then an angel. He was excited about the treats, but mostly he wanted to be a good boy.

And revel in Abbale calling him by two endearments in a row.

He was too excited to sit down, so he texted Christy.

Levi: Merry Christmas!

Levi: I forgot to tell Daddy that I bought treats, but he says that maybe I can still earn them.

He sent her the same picture.

She called back a moment later, jumping right into the conversation. "OMG. Did he say you could tell me about it, though?"

"Yep! Nothing too personal, but he knows you're my best friend. And treats aren't personal, right? Like, you're going to see me do this every time I get a coffee."

"You lucky dog." Christy sighed.

"You're just impatient. Saul already sent an email to Javier with all the details. I still think you should ambush Nikhil at the airport, cuff him, and take him home."

"Nope. And don't rush me. Nikhil needs time to get used to things."

"Nikhil needs whips and chains."

"Yes, but that's after I lure him into my lair."

He grinned. He knew she took Nikhil very seriously, but if she was joking, that meant she was feeling confident. "With whips and chains."

"I plan to have a very professional meeting about dating in the workplace."

"Just saying… you can have that meeting while he's bent over your lap. I mean, it worked for me." He was only partially joking. He knew that Christy would handle things responsibly, and she had a much more complicated situation to work through, since he was her direct supervisor and Nikhil was going to be shy. But the teasing would build her confidence.

"I'm going to tell your Daddy to give you extra spankings for that."

"Please!"

There was a pause. "So are you happy?"

"I can't even tell you how much. It's like… OK, this is going to sound stupid, but he doesn't get annoyed with me. I know that's a low bar, but he, like, when I do something silly or ridiculous, I think it actually makes him happy. I mean, maybe he'll change his mind later, but…"

"Nope," Christy cut in. "Don't go down that path. He knows you already. He smiles every time he sees you. Especially when you're doing something dumb."

"Hey! I didn't say dumb."

"If it helps, you make me smile, too."

"Awww."

"Just be yourself. Remember the rule?"

"Let Daddy set the limits."

"Yep. And how's that going so far?"

"Oh, God. It's heavenly. He gets to order food for me and I have to ask for permission for treats. Except today, but that was a special circumstance because it's Chinese food for Christmas. But otherwise he says he's going to spoil me."

"Good for you. That's exactly what you need."

"You're never going to give Nikhil anything, are you?"

"I might deign to give him my attention if he's very lucky."

He didn't quite understand how Christy could be so warm when they were all working together, but so harshly cold with Nikhil sometimes. Yet the sexual tension between them practically crackled in the air. Nikhil was just begging to be ground under her sneakers.

Not his kink, but he knew a good match when he saw one.

And he was starting to wonder if Christy's relationship with Nikhil might look different from what she'd had in the past. The way she talked about him was just different. When she wasn't joking, she was usually sweet and concerned, and he'd never heard her talk about any other sub that way.

"Oh, hang on." Christy said something he couldn't make out and then returned. "Gotta go. About to start Christmas dinner."

"It's barely even lunch time."

"Yes, but it's Christmas *dinner*."

"Got it. Can you have it for breakfast?"

"No. That's Christmas breakfast. It's, like, danishes from a package and little personal boxes of cereal for the kids because no one wants to cook two meals on the same day. Oh, and oranges for some reason. It's a time-honored tradition."

"Enjoy your dinner!"

"Enjoy your Chinese food!"

"Love you. Bye!"

"Bye!"

He put his phone back in his pocket, still smiling. He put on some danceable music and wandered around his apartment picking up a few mislaid objects and taking the Chinese food out of the bag.

When the doorbell buzzed, he raced to answer it.

"Daddy!" He tackled Saul with a hug.

Daddy laughed. "You're like an overgrown puppy."

"Is that bad?" He was pretty sure it wasn't now.

"Nope. It's adorable." Daddy pulled him down for a kiss. Kissing involved a lot of bending over on his part and looking up on Daddy's part, but if Daddy didn't mind, he didn't either.

Plus, if his back got sore, there could be kissing on the couch, or the bed, or the floor, or… yeah, kissing just like this, with Daddy cupping his cheeks and lingering over his lips. Yeah, this was just fine.

"So, tell me about your grand plan."

Levi dragged him into the living room, pointing to each object. "Chinese food. Movies. Couch. Daddy."

"Sounds good. What are we watching? Wait… are we watching Hanukkah movies?"

"OMG. I didn't even think of that. *Are* there even Hanukkah movies? Christy asked me that and I just assumed that there weren't, but what if there *are?*"

"I have no idea. It seemed like something you would know."

"It seems like something my *phone* would know." Levi settled onto the couch. When Saul sat down next to him, he wriggled around until Daddy was snuggling him from behind, looking over his shoulder.

"OK, here's a list. 'Eight Hanukkah movies that will light up your holiday.'"

He scrolled down and they both reeled back when they saw the first one.

"*An American Tale?*" Levi couldn't get over it. "Everyone's favorite children's movie about escaping the Holocaust. Happy Hanukkah everybody!"

He scrolled to the next one, and read the blurb.

"Hang on," Saul stopped him. "Adam Sandler made a *movie* about the Hanukkah Song?"

"OMG. It's an hour and a half long. What's even in it?"

"Keep going."

"OK, um, a Hanukkah sports movie about middle schoolers. A private detective spoof? Have you ever heard of *The Hebrew Hammer?* Ooh! The next one actually says that Vanity Fair named it 'the worst film of any trilogy to appear in a movie theater.' This is epic! OK, a rom com, *Hitched for the Holidays.* Could be OK. They're straight."

Saul pointed to the next one. "Look! They're gay! There's a gay Hanukkah movie. *Call Me By Your Name.* We're watching that."

"Done. Do you want to see what else is on the list?"

"Go for it."

"Ummm… the description says this movie isn't even about Hanukkah, but they wanted eight and one of the neighbors is Jewish. Now that's just sad."

"Well, now we know."

Levi flicked back to the search. "Um…. it looks like there are a couple more rom coms out there. Like, straight ones. And a couple comedies. And… no way. A horror movie. It's about… wait for it… the Hanukiller. So…"

"Tell me we're not watching that."

"God, no. I hate horror movies. They make me all jumpy. And the plots are terrible. But, we have discovered that there are enough Hanukkah movies for a full-day marathon."

Daddy scowled at him. "Your limit is three."

"You mean I don't get to watch"–he flipped back to find the most outrageous one–"*Full-Court Miracle?*" That was the middle school basketball flick.

"Three."

He pouted. Not because he wanted to watch more than three movies, but because he *could*. Because his Daddy didn't mind him being outrageous.

Levi clicked on the link to start the movie they chose, but then paused it. "This is a foreign film. They're speaking Italian."

"Is that a bad thing?"

"It's going to be sad. And it's summer time, so it's not exactly Hanukkah. Why was this even here?"

"We don't have to watch it."

"No, I want to. I just need to know *how* sad it's going to be. Let's get some food."

"I'll get it for you, motek. Thank you for ordering." Saul kissed his cheek and urged him off his lap. He was getting the *motek* nickname all the time now, and it was even better than *boy*. His own special name.

Levi read the synopsis. "OK, it's sad," he called out to the kitchen.

"Did you just read the whole plot?"

"Yep. Want me to tell you?"

"Absolutely not. I want to enjoy the movie."

"Well, sometimes you can enjoy the movie *more* if you know why it's going to be sad."

Saul came back with their plates and set them on the coffee table. "You're precious." He grabbed Levi's chin and gave him a lingering kiss. "Now let's celebrate Christmas properly."

Levi snorted.

They started out sitting up so they could eat, but as soon as he was done, Levi draped himself over Saul's lap.

Call Me By Your Name was indeed sad. But it was also beautiful and poignant and touching, like a good foreign film should be.

"That was amazing." Levi stretched and curled into Daddy's arms. "We need something cheerful now, though."

"Good point. I don't think I can sit for any longer, though. I need to move around."

They put the leftovers away and stretched their legs. Saul was washing their two plates and Levi hugged him from behind. He carefully kept his hands below Saul's chest, since he knew it could be an uncomfortable area of his body.

"Abbale?"

"Hmmmm?"

"I'm really happy."

Daddy put a hand over his. It was wet and maybe a little soapy, but it didn't matter. "I'm glad to hear it. Though I may have been cheating a little with the letters you left in Cuffd. I don't know what I'm going to do when I run out of hints."

"Oh, don't worry. I'll let you know what I want."

"I'm sure you will." Daddy laughed.

Levi pulled back. "Am I too greedy?" He was thinking of the boy in the film. He'd been a little bit pushy, and he'd only gotten what he wanted for a few days. It left him thinking about glorious things that came to a tragic end.

Saul gave him a searching look. What was he thinking?

"Let's go talk on the couch, baby boy." Saul was smiling as he reached out his hand, but Levi didn't want to take it.

Levi had been checking in sure, but he'd expected the answer to be *no*. He'd hoped that Saul was finally the Daddy who didn't think he was too much. Who didn't need to have a "conversation" with him about his behavior.

This had suddenly gone from the most relaxing, perfect day to the worst. He felt like he had rocks in his stomach.

"Come on," Saul coaxed. "This isn't a bad thing."

Yeah, sure.

When Levi didn't move, Saul tugged at his hand. He reluctantly let himself be led back to the living room.

Saul patted his lap, but Levi didn't feel like he could sit there. He wasn't sure if he could trust what it meant. And maybe he wasn't sure if he deserved it.

Saul was looking up at him with such care though. And he wanted to deserve it. He wanted it so desperately. He was sure he could change a little bit. That was part of letting Daddy set the limits, right?

Saul started to look a little worried and Levi realized that he was hovering over him. He always felt uncomfortable being so tall and forcing people to crane their necks. With Saul looking up at him with those frowning brows, it was horribly awkward, but he still couldn't make it to his lap.

He wet his lips. "May I?" He indicated the ground.

"May you what?"

"May I kneel?" He wasn't used to kneeling. Most of the time, well really all of the time, he'd rather be on Daddy's lap. But right now, he needed to break from their familiar roles. To feel the subservience of the gesture deep in his core.

"You may."

It felt like a benediction. He fell to the ground in a tangle of limbs, hitting his knee on the table leg.

He rubbed it, glaring at the coffee table. "Ow."

Saul chuckled. "Come here, boy." He patted his thigh.

Levi scrambled over and rested his head gratefully. He wasn't really kneeling, but he sort of was, and hopefully Saul would still think it was OK. It was kind of a compromise.

Saul ran his fingers through his hair. It was heavenly, even if he didn't deserve it. He felt warm and protected in that small space. Saul's skin was warm through the denim, and he wanted to nuzzle in closer, to where his soft t-shirt met his thighs.

"Is your knee alright?"

Levi wrinkled his nose. "Yeah. I'm not very good at kneeling, I guess."

"No," Saul commented in amusement. "I don't suppose you are."

"Is that bad?"

Saul traced along the back of his neck, sending shivers down his spine. "It's very Levi."

"Is that bad, then?"

Saul sighed.

Oh. That was a very bad sign. Levi was too clumsy and tall and confident again. Too *greedy* when he should have been happy with what he already had.

"Baby? Motek? Can you please look at me?"

He didn't want to, but Saul was still his Daddy. At least for now.

He looked up.

Saul hooked one hand around the back of his neck, the other under his chin. It was a possessive hold, one that let him know exactly who was in control and exactly what was expected of him. It went straight to his cock. Made him want to do anything just to please him.

Saul's eyes smoldered. For a long time they just looked at each other.

When Saul finally spoke, his voice was deep and measured. "You are not greedy."

The statement was so simple, yet communicated so powerfully, that it took Levi a moment to understand it. He opened his mouth to object, but Saul put a finger over his lips.

"I want you to listen to me, boy. First, whoever told you that you were greedy was an asshole. Probably a greedy asshole, but let's not worry about that now."

Levi didn't say anything. It had been, well, a lot of guys. Even Christy said it, though she said it with affection.

"Second, what does it mean to be greedy? Give me a definition."

"Um… I think I'm…"

"Nope. This isn't 'I statements.' A person is greedy when they…"

"…want everything for themselves and don't think about other people."

"Mmmm-hmmmm. So, let's go through some examples. I brought you a ridiculously sugary drink because you asked for it in your adorable Santa letter. And the next day *you* went to the coffee shop and texted me because… "

What was he getting at? "I texted you because… oh, shit. I was supposed to ask you about getting a treat."

"No, baby. We hadn't established that yet. You texted me because you were buying a coffee for Christy and yourself, and you asked me very sweetly if you could get me one, too. Why did you do that?"

"I just… I was feeling so happy and I wanted you to be happy, too." It had seemed pretty self-explanatory at the time. He hadn't even thought about it beyond imagining the smile on Saul's face. That was kind of like a treat in itself.

"Alright, and how about ordering food? We agreed that I would do all the ordering, didn't we? Because we both enjoy knowing that I'm taking care of you?"

"Yeah…"

"But you were really excited today to pick up something from your favorite place, so you ordered our lunch, right? Why was that?"

"Um, because I thought you would like it and I wanted to share my favorite things. So I forgot the rules, but I *promise* I can do better."

"Sweetheart, you're missing the point." Saul looked frustrated. "Dammit, boy," he finally snapped. "Come up here so that I can hold you."

That made it so much easier. Levi was even less convinced now that he deserved to be in Daddy's lap, but that just made him want it more. And if Daddy said so, he had to obey.

He sat in his favorite position, knees on either side of Daddy's thighs with their chests pressed together. He curled into Saul's neck, breathing in the scent of his skin. Feeling Daddy's disappointment was *terrible*.

Saul spoke softly against his cheek. "I think I'm not doing a very good job of this. I want to try again." He took a deep breath and let it out. "I don't think that you're greedy. I think that you're exuberant and I love watching you ask for, or even demand, what you want and need."

Really?

"I never thought about being a Daddy until I read your letters, but I have to say that so far, it's a hundred times better than what I was expecting. I. Like. Taking. Care. Of. You." He gave Levi's shoulder a little shake to punctuate each word. As if he could shake the meaning into his brain.

"When you tell me what you want," he continued, "it makes it feel easy and natural for me to be able to give it to you. I don't have to guess how to make you happy, and I think it's an exhilarating feeling for both of us. You like asking for things and I like giving them to you because it's hot as fuck, but also because it feels right. Do you understand?"

"I want to." He really did. Because what Daddy was saying sounded perfect. It was what he'd always thought having a Daddy was supposed to be like. It just hadn't been true before.

"The thing is, baby, I can keep telling you that you're not greedy. I recall that we had a long talk about it yesterday, and I'm happy to say it a million more times if you need me to. But *you* have to believe it."

Levi soaked up all of Saul's warm caresses, but he still shook his head. "Even Christy says that I'm greedy."

Saul was quiet for a minute. Thinking. "What does Christy say about it?"

"She says I'm the greediest boy so I need a Daddy who can spoil me."

"Is that a bad thing when she says it?"

"Not from her perspective. But then, she's into all sorts of things like humiliation and cuckolding and high-protocol service that are pretty much the opposite of that, so I don't know if she understands."

"I think she understands you and your needs pretty well, actually. She's still a Domme and I'm sure that she has other ways of spoiling her subs that fit their needs. She's your best friend, so maybe she knows what she's talking about. Let me ask it another way. Do you want to be greedy?"

"I… Yeah. I do, I guess. It's just… I don't want to be selfish. Like, I really do care about other people."

"Ahhhhh…" It sounded like Daddy had some kind of revelation, but Levi couldn't figure it out. "Would Christy say that you're selfish?"

"Um, I don't think so. We split things pretty equally, and we take care of each other, I think."

"So is being greedy different from being selfish?"

Levi finally looked up. He had no idea. Didn't they mean the same thing?

Daddy gave him a soft kiss. "Let's redefine those terms. At least for our relationship. *Selfish* is when you put yourself first and don't think or care about other people. I would say that you're selfish about… maybe zero percent of the time. In fact, you're one of the least selfish people I know. You really delight in making other people happy.

"Levi, I can't even tell you how many things I've done with you this week that have made me so happy that I couldn't stop smiling. I never thought I'd enjoy dancing at a club, but I had an amazing time. I've never had anyone ask me so sincerely if they could bring me something as simple as a coffee just because they wanted me to be happy. I can't even tell you how much that meant to me, that we would have that as part of our dynamic."

Saul paused, as if overcome with some emotion. "I also… I also didn't think that I'd feel comfortable doing anything sexual with you where I had an orgasm or exposed more of my body, at least not for a while. You've given me a huge gift of feeling comfortable with my own anatomy, largely because you were so selfless that you begged me to feel good, too, during our scene yesterday."

"I… really? I did all that? I mean… I'm not aiming for false modesty. I just didn't see it that way." But if he had done that for Saul, that was kind of awesome. He had no idea Saul had been so nervous. He found himself starting to smile.

"Well, that's always how I've seen you. Generous, dedicated, supportive of other people, and constantly sharing the things that you enjoy to make other people happy. Since we've been in this relationship, I've seen it blossom even more."

"I… wow. I… I really didn't see myself that way."

This was a whole new world. Not just empty promises. Saul had really thought about this.

"It's true." Saul gave him a deep, lingering kiss, and this time he let himself luxuriate in it. He was starting to see what he meant and… Well, if he thought of himself outside of his needs from a Daddy, it wasn't a bad description of him, he was pretty sure.

"Now let's talk about that other word that you've been throwing around. We're going to say that *greedy* means that you're stepping into the role of being my boy and letting me take care of you. Greedy means that you get so excited about sharing something special with me, or letting me give you a treat, that you can't wait to tell me about it. Greedy means that you give me ideas about how I can make you happy, and then you share that happiness with me so that we both benefit. And if that's what greedy is for us, then I want you to be greedy all the time."

"Is that… is that really what you want?"

"Absolutely. I can't get enough of my greedy boy. My neshama."

Levi beamed. He was a greedy boy, and he was Saul's *soul*. Even if it didn't quite mean the same thing across the languages, it was the most beautiful of all the nicknames. The one he'd been waiting for.

"So, let's go through those examples again." Daddy looked determined, and Levi was more than willing to let him do it. He needed to know that it was really true.

"You asked for a coffee and when I gave it to you, you clapped your hands, looked adorable as fuck when you thanked me, and then moaned like a porn star when you finally tasted it. Greedy or selfish?"

Saul pressed a finger to his lips to stop him from answering. He was coming to love that gesture. It was so sweet, and just such a *Daddy* thing to do. Daddy wanted him to think about something before he spoke, and that meant a lot to him.

"When you got that coffee, were you thinking about how much you enjoy coffee, or how much you enjoyed receiving a gift from me?"

"Definitely the second one. I mean, I can buy my own coffee. And, um, it was too hot to actually drink so I just pretended to sip it."

Daddy's eyes sparkled. "I had wondered about that. Mine was still way too hot when I got back to my office. So, selfish or greedy? Did you want the coffee, or did you want to share a special moment with your Daddy?"

"Um, greedy, I guess."

"There we go. How about begging me to take you dancing? Greedy or selfish?"

"Um… I didn't know at the time that you didn't like dancing. I wouldn't have asked if you did."

"And I would have missed out on a fun evening. But I think you're proving my point that it was…"

"Greedy. You know, it's really weird thinking of the word that way. Like it's a good thing."

"Oh, it's a very good thing. One of my favorite things about our relationship. OK, here's another one. How about when I told you that you could only watch three movies. I recall you pouting at me. Tell me what you were thinking. Selfish or greedy?"

"Um… I don't think I actually wanted to watch more than three movies. Like, I don't even care if we watch another one or not. I just wanted to, uh, I don't even know how to explain it. Have your attention? See if you would tell me no? Neither of those make sense."

"So… what you're saying is that you wanted me to demonstrate to you that I'm your Daddy and that I was going to set limits, because it's a routine that we both enjoy. Selfish or greedy?"

"Greedy, I guess?"

"That's right, baby. Here's the thing I notice about you. I don't think that you need a Daddy to help you manage your everyday life or meet your goals. You're already doing an excellent job of that on your own. What you need a Daddy for is making sure that you're adored and spoiled, and giving you some limits because it makes you feel cared for and secure. Does that sound about right?"

It did. No one else had ever understood it so clearly. "Yes, Daddy."

"And since you don't need me to help you reach actual goals or set actual limits, you're finding ways to invent them. When you make sure that you have all of my attention, when you act up, and when you tell me what you want, that's how you communicate what's important in our relationship. It's not being selfish and putting yourself first. It's you being a greedy boy to make sure that I get to be the doting Daddy who's lucky enough to be able to spoil you."

"And you really want that? It isn't silly?"

Daddy nuzzled his nose. "It's silly and adorable and I want it more than anything."

"Thank you, Abbale." He couldn't think of a more sincere way to say it than with his special name. "I don't know what I did to deserve a Daddy as wonderful as you."

"As long as you know that you *do* deserve this, that's all that I want. And the next time that you request something, I want you to ask yourself if you're being selfish or greedy. If you want something for yourself, or if you're doing your part to build up the Daddy/boy relationship for both of us."

"I will, Daddy." It was an easy promise to make, but he still needed another minute to think. He relaxed back into Daddy's shoulder. *Greedy* and *selfish* were just two silly words, but the distinction between them was earth-shattering.

"I'd like to hold you for a while, now." Daddy's soothing hands drifted up and down his back.

Levi snuggled in, soaking in all of the comfort. When he was being greedy he was *building* something. And that changed everything.

"Do you want to watch another movie, motek?"

"Sure."

He heard the TV flick on behind him, though Daddy quickly lowered the volume of whatever trailer started auto-playing. "Maybe one of the rom coms we were looking at earlier? I think we need something light."

"Sure," he murmured happily. "You choose."

There was silence for a while, then music and a low hum of voices filled the room.

"Do you want to turn around and watch it?"

Levi shook his head, his cheek rubbing against Daddy's ear and his chin pressed to the back of the couch. "I want to watch it like this."

Daddy chuckled. "That might not be very efficient."

"I'm being greedy." He tested out saying it.

Daddy nuzzled against his ear. "Good boy." Those gentle hands kept stroking his back.

There were more movie noises from across the room. Singing. Something with cars. People laughing. Levi relaxed with Daddy's arms keeping him safe.

"Baby? My simcha?"

"Hmmm?" He didn't want to think about anything. He just wanted more nicknames.

"You mentioned a fantasy about the couch before. Is this it?"

Levi nodded. Maybe there was something that he wanted more. If he told Abbale, would he give it to him?

He was so close to Daddy's ear that he didn't have to speak much louder than a whisper. "This is one variation."

"Will you tell me about all of them?"

"Um… they all start kind of like this. My Daddy"– he pressed a kiss to Saul's neck–"is holding me on the couch. Sometimes we're sitting like this, or laying down on our sides, or I'm turned around the other way. And sometimes this is the whole fantasy. I'm just floating here and my Daddy is holding me."

"Do you ever watch the movie?"

"Sometimes. At least at first. But it's more of a prop."

"What are the other variations?"

"Sometimes you would touch me. Like you weren't even paying attention to me, but I would just get more and more turned on, until I was ready to explode. And you would just tell me to watch the movie."

Saul hummed in appreciation. "Would I let you come?"

"Sometimes. By the time it happened it would be like lightning. But sometimes I would just kind of drift off into this sleepy-sexy place and never come. I imagine that when I want to fall asleep."

"Like the other day when I called you?"

He nodded into Daddy's neck. He wasn't sure if he was feeling shy or coy, but it was easier to talk about while he was hiding.

"Ah. Are there other variations?"

"So many. I mean, sometimes you'd make me wear a butt plug or a cock ring. Or a cock *cage* during the whole thing. And just act like we were just watching a movie while I was going crazy."

"You've really thought about this."

"The couch is my favorite part of the apartment. I take naps out here a lot."

"And touch yourself while you do."

"Obviously."

"Any other variations?"

"Sometimes…" Huh. Now he wasn't sure if he should share this.

"Yeah?"

He pulled back so he could watch Daddy's face. "I'm not sure if I can say this in the right way. Because I don't want to pressure you. And I am also really, really excited about whatever parts of your body you want to share, and really, really OK if you don't want to do anything like this."

"Thank you for considering that. It does make a difference to me that you're thinking about it, but I think we'll be able to do almost anything, even if I need some time to work up to it. As long as you're OK with that."

"Abbale, I'm very, very greedy about getting to make you feel good."

Saul gave him a soft kiss. "Thank you, my simcha. That means a lot to me. Now, tell me about these fantasies."

"Well, sometimes you would sit on the couch watching the movie. And I would… keep your cock warm for you."

"Oh? And how would you do that?"

"Well, you might pull me over and just put my mouth on it. Like, maybe with your pants on at first, and then after a while you'd open the zipper. And I could just hold it like that in my mouth for the whole movie.

"Or sometimes, you would tell me to prep myself and I would just… sit there. With your cock inside me. And you would talk about the movie, and every time you would laugh or move a little bit it would just, like, nail my prostate but I wouldn't be allowed to move or anything."

"Sweetheart, you have the most wonderful ideas."

Phew. He'd been worried that he'd offend or worry Saul by talking about parts of his body that were a little different, especially after what he'd said before.

"So, is there a particular one you want to try?"

Levi shook his head. "The whole point is that Daddy chooses. Is that…?" He was about to ask if it was greedy. But of course it *was* greedy. And Daddy wanted that.

"Was that a question?"

"No. That was me being greedy." He grinned. "I want you to choose."

"Well," Daddy drew the word out, "in that case, I want you naked, prepped, and back here with a plug in that cute little hole."

"Really?"

Daddy nodded, his eyes already fixed on the screen. "Mmmm-hmmmm. I'll let you know what you miss."

As if he cared about the movie at all. Daddy was absolutely nailing this.

He got ready in record time, and when he returned Daddy hadn't moved from his seat at the far end of the couch. Actually… there were some glasses and drinks on the coffee table, so clearly he had moved at least once. But you wouldn't know by looking at him. He looked completely absorbed in the show.

Daddy was taking care of him and his heart melted all over again.

"Hey," he offered, not quite sure how to start the scene. Should he just walk over and sit down? Do something seductive? Pretend he wasn't *totally naked except for a butt plug?*

"Oh, hey babe. Come on over," Daddy patted his lap, but his eyes had already returned to the screen. "You didn't miss much. They're going over to the guys' parents house, but they're trying not to act like they're together so he doesn't lose the bet with his brother."

It was a good thing that Levi didn't care about this movie because it sounded inane. Who thought up these things?

Levi crossed the room and Daddy helped him settle onto the couch, his back propped up against the arm while his feet trailed over the next cushion. With each step, the plug jostled inside him, sending jolts of pleasure through him.

When he got into place, his bare ass was nestled between Daddy's thighs, the base of the plug pressing against one of Daddy's jeans-clad legs. It felt wickedly indecent.

Also, Daddy was hard. Oh, God, that was hot. Whatever secret plans Daddy had carried out while Levi was getting ready, they involved Daddy's cock.

Even if they didn't do anything with it today, just feeling it pressed against his thigh made his mouth water.

"That's the guy's mother," Saul pointed out. "There's a running gag with those cookies she's holding. Nobody likes them."

Fuck. They were starting. They were really doing this.

Even while Saul was talking, he was already caressing Levi in long sweeping strokes. Down his chest, over his belly, across his hip, and then down to his knees. He didn't make any effort to touch his cock, but he didn't avoid it either.

Of course, Levi had already been half hard just from fingering himself open to get the plug in, and now that he was here, finally, with his real, actual Daddy, his cock was pointing straight up in the air.

Saul ran his hand back up, his wrist gliding over his dick as it passed.

"Oh, are you cold, motek?" Daddy asked.

"A little bit," he admitted. That aspect of being naked in the living room hadn't occurred to him before.

Daddy drew his favorite blanket from the back of the couch and draped it over him, taking special care to keep his feet warm.

Then, under the blanket, the long, slow caresses resumed. He felt shivery and small. Daddy had gotten the balance just right. It didn't feel like *he* was being ignored. Daddy was clearly happy that he was here, enjoying the opportunity to snuggle and watch a movie together.

What Daddy was ignoring was this intense need pulsing through him. The desire to accommodate and submit himself to whatever Daddy needed, just to please him. The glorious flashes of pleasure that the plug sent through him and the sporadic thrill of Daddy touching his cock, however incidentally.

"Warm enough?" Daddy asked.

It took him a moment to find his voice. "Yes, Abbale."

"Good. I've got *you* to keep me nice and cozy, but I don't want your feet to get cold."

Levi let his eyes drift closed. He'd never felt so warm and cared for in his life. He could almost feel the warmth like it was an emotion. Like the intimacy and his favorite blanket were wrapping around him together, their heat intertwined.

Daddy put an arm behind his shoulders and pulled him over so that he could rest his head more on Daddy's chest than the couch. That was even better.

For a while, Daddy just rubbed up and down his leg, fingers skimming within an inch of his balls but never quite touching.

Daddy laughed at something on the screen and the vibrations sent another wave of need through him as the plug shifted. Daddy looked down at him and smiled, like they were sharing the joke from the movie.

Yeah, the movie. With, um, some people in it. All he could think about was the angle of Daddy's jaw and the kissable little lines at the corner of his eyes. He didn't need to see anything else.

After some interminable time, Daddy's hands started to rove, finally settling on Levi's cock. But not his whole cock. Daddy was just holding him loosely, fingers curled right below the head. Then he started to run his thumb gently over the frenulum, swiping gently from side to side.

It took about two of those soft strokes before Levi was ready to come. He'd already been crazy with desire and that little notch was so tender and sensitive.

He sucked in a breath and held it.

Oh, fuck. Daddy was still watching the movie, thumb massaging slowly and rhythmically like he didn't even know he was doing it. He could just as well have been rubbing Levi's hand or his knee, but instead he was calmly brushing across the center of all of Levi's arousal.

Levi whimpered. Loudly. It was just too good. Too intense and sweet and perfect.

"You OK, honey?" Daddy didn't move his hand, but he paused while he spoke.

That was the only reason Levi was able to talk. "Mmm-hmmm. Great."

"Oh, good." Daddy resumed that maddening caress. He nodded toward the TV. "Oh, this is the *other* brother. He knows what's going on, but he says he's not going to tell anyone. I personally think he's going to be the one to screw it up, though."

Yeah. Sure. Whatever. Because at that moment, Saul

switched to thumbing down his slit. Levi was leaking what seemed like gallons of precum, so Daddy's thumb slid around easily, as he worked his way across and just inside that tiny hole.

Oh, fuck. *Fuck.* He always loved that sensation, but usually it was mingled with a dozen more. Kissing and caressing, and definitely, definitely more stimulation to the rest of his dick.

It was just so... focused. Like a laser. He'd thought that the last spot was the most sensitive, but this, right here? The sheer pleasure of the light touch was almost punishing. Especially when Daddy pressed in just a little deeper, awakening nerve endings he hadn't even known were there. There was something just so gloriously wrong about being penetrated there, even a centimeter, that called out to everything in his submissive side.

Levi started shaking. He couldn't help it.

He was *dying* of erogenous need and Daddy was just watching the screen.

He needed... he needed... something more. Or something else. Something to just balance that tight, inescapable precision. Except that moving shook the plug, and now he was rocking back and forth between two narrow points of pleasure.

Daddy gave him a soft kiss on his forehead. His expression held only fond concern. "How are you doing, my neshama?" As if the stuttering moans coming out of his mouth were something unexpected.

He nodded, knowing that if he opened his mouth he'd do nothing but scream.

"We should try sounding some time," Daddy commented offhandedly. "I think you'd like it." Then he turned back to the TV.

Levi was never going to make it out of this alive. More importantly, he wasn't going to last another minute without coming.

"Da– Daddy?"

"Hmmm, my motek?" He didn't even look up from the screen.

"Daddy, please. Need to come."

"No, baby. Watch the movie."

There it was. Levi's heart was already beating out of his chest, but now it doubled. *Watch the movie.* Daddy wanted him to watch the movie.

He tilted his head blindly toward the screen. The couple was kissing to a big swell of music that was probably the turning point of the whole movie. Ironic how tame and distant it felt in comparison to Daddy positively owning every need and sensation in Levi's body.

Daddy's thumb never strayed from that small area, just drifted around the tip of the head and then slithered into the slit again.

Dual pleasure washed over him, and the only thing he could think of was *not coming.* He had to wait. Because Daddy told him to.

Or, oh God. Was Daddy ever going to tell him to come?

He hadn't said later or not yet. He'd just said no.

There had to be a lot more to the movie. There were… lots of people talking at a party or something. And all Daddy was doing was rubbing his thumb in a little circle and watching.

Don't come, he told himself. *Daddy doesn't want you to come.*

Daddy wiggled his thumb in to that impossibly tiny opening and his senses overloaded.

Don't come. Don't come for Daddy.

Daddy added a little slide of his wrist, just enough to make the hot skin on his cock glide over the shaft.

Daddy says can't come.

He needed. He was burning. He was dying.

Don't come.

Some deeper level of pleasure welled up inside him. Not from his cock or his desperate prostate, but something bigger. Something too large to contain. It started in his chest, and then expanded until it filled up every corner of his lax body.

Don't come.

It grew beyond his boundaries.

Don't come.

Daddy was going to torture him with pleasure and he was just going to take it. To do nothing but exist for his Daddy's pleasure. It wasn't a thought that came in words, just a profound sense of knowing.

Don't come.

He belonged to Daddy.

The world fell away.

There was only Daddy's breath. Daddy's hand. Daddy's shoulders and arms holding him close.

Those were the only things he needed.

And they were his.

He didn't even remember closing his eyes as that swell of rapture lifted him away.

17

SAUL

Saul slowly drew his hand away from Levi's still hard cock.

His boy didn't even stir.

For a long time, Saul couldn't move either. He just felt… awed. Levi was deep, deep into subspace, and Saul had put him there.

He gathered him up into a more comfortable position, prepared to wait as long as he needed to.

Some people entered subspace easily and some never at all. He didn't know where Levi ran on that scale. But even if it was a welcome and ready place for him, the sheer amount of trust that it demonstrated broke something open inside of Saul and set it free.

That's when he knew he was in love. Maybe he'd been falling in love since that first interview, when Levi had made buttplug jokes and helped him pick out his new name. He'd probably known it when he'd gone out into the rain for that over-sugared peppermint drink. But this was the moment when it really hit him.

Levi was vulnerable and sweet and silly. But more, his absolute conviction in what he needed in a Daddy had led Saul to discover some important things about who he could be.

In just a few days, Levi had shown him that not only could he be man enough to be Levi's boyfriend, but that everything Levi wanted in a Daddy was exactly who he wanted to be.

He still didn't think he was the perfect Daddy, at least not in an abstract sense. Maybe in Levi's eyes.

But they were a perfect fit together.

He felt Levi shift in his arms and drew him closer. "How are you doing, sweetheart?"

Levi blinked up at him. "Daddy?"

"I'm here, my neshama."

"Mmmmm… hold me."

"Always." It was definitely too soon to promise anything. But he could store up the sentiments until the right time. Knowing Levi, he would probably blurt it out when neither of them were expecting it anyway.

He leaned forward to snag the glass of water from the coffee table. He'd gotten a few things ready while Levi was in the bathroom, giving him plenty of time to plan the scene.

"Water?"

Levi looked surprised, then seemed to identify the cup in front of him. He opened his mouth and Saul helped him drink, both of them holding the glass together.

"I brought over the mango juice, too, if you want some."

Levi started to shake his head.

"The sugar would be good for you."

He nodded.

It took a bit more maneuvering, but Saul got the mango juice poured into the other glass and lifted it to Levi's lips.

"Thank you, Daddy. That's good."

"Well, you deserve lots of treats. You were beautiful for me. My simcha." That was what Levi was. His joy.

Levi nuzzled against his chest. "That was so good I can't even believe it was real."

"Was it as good as your fantasies?"

"A thousand times better."

"Is this what you're going to expect every time that we watch a movie now?"

Levi grinned up at him. "Every time."

"Greedy, needy boy," Saul told him fondly.

Levi smiled back, but it was interrupted by a yawn.

"Do you want to go take a real nap?"

"Don't want to move. Nap here."

That was probably part of the fantasy, but it would likely get uncomfortable quickly. "What if I held you in bed?"

"Mmmm… OK."

Saul eased them both up and guided Levi toward the bedroom. After he pulled back the covers, Levi collapsed on the mattress. He held out a desperate arm when Saul stepped away.

"Shhhhh… my motek. I'm just getting the blankets sorted. And I need to take out your plug."

He gently worked out the stiff silicone and tossed it into the bathroom sink to clean later. Right now, he needed to be back with his boy. In the bedroom, he shucked off most of his clothes.

Levi's eyes were already closed, so he risked taking off his binder, which had been killing his ribs today, and then slipping his t-shirt back on. The exposure made him uncomfortable in a different way, but he couldn't exactly sleep with it on all the time. And he intended to sleep next to Levi a lot.

Trust.

He might not be comfortable with his own body, but he had to trust that Levi could handle it.

When he got down to his briefs, he debated taking off the harness and packer, or maybe slipping out the flexible rod inside.

It was going to be uncomfortable to sleep in. It was probably stupid but… he wanted Levi to know that he was just as hard and horny from their scene as Levi still clearly was. He wanted to hold Levi and feel his own cock rubbing up against Levi's firm body. If his anatomy fully reflected how he felt, this is what it would look like.

He walked around to the other side of the bed and drew back the covers.

"Daddy." Levi rolled over onto him, lazily kissing

the nearest bit of flesh, which happened to be his collar bone. "Want to make you feel good, too." His voice was slurred and syrupy, just like that first phone call.

"You did, baby. You do."

"Please Abbale? I just… kisses? Or…" he drew Saul's fingers to his lips and started to suck. Fuck, that was erotic. Saul could just imagine him on his cock.

That's what it felt like. Like a blowjob. A leisurely, decadent blowjob, all soft lips and eager tongue.

Levi pulled Saul's fingers out to speak. "Daddy, I'm greedy for you. Please let me."

Saul wondered if getting his Daddy off was part of the kink for Levi, a form of service and devotion. This was the third time he'd requested it, and he didn't describe it as reciprocating. He described it as being greedy.

All three times he'd been floating on endorphins, and all three times he'd begged.

He didn't specify what he was begging for this time. Maybe because he was being thoughtful about Saul's body. Maybe because he wanted it to be Daddy's choice.

Another treat that he could give to his greedy boy.

How could he say no to such an innocent, generous offer? The question really, was how. He loved the idea of Levi falling asleep while suckling on his fingers. Both of them dreaming, maybe, that it was his cock.

But he also knew how much Levi would enjoy seeing him come. His greedy, *selfless* boy.

He withdrew his fingers from Levi's warm, inviting mouth and took his hand.

Wordlessly, he drew Levi's hand down his body. Over the wrinkles in his t-shirt, down the narrow strip of skin that exposed his treasure trail.

And finally, after another moment to make sure he was ready, under the waistband of his briefs.

He kept his hand tight over Levi's, letting him know that he would be directing all of the action.

When, together, they reached the tip of his cock, he heard Levi's breath catch.

"Daddy," he whispered, awe in his voice.

He knew what Levi would feel. The smooth head warmed from his body, a hard length with detailed veins and soft skin sliding over it. Now that he had Levi's cock to compare it with, he was even more impressed with the craftsmanship, because, yeah, it was pretty realistic.

He wondered if someone touching it, maybe who didn't know, would even realize that it was manufactured instead of grown. He'd used dildos before, but they were always, purposefully, completely unrealistic. In his mind, he'd always veered away from something that he wanted a bit too much but still might not be enough.

This one he'd bought because he wanted it to feel like an extension of his own body. Something that someone could just look at and see him as a man, despite the straps that slung over the wrinkled balls and around his waist. He thought it looked pretty good in the mirror, and, yeah, he'd tried jerking off with his hand around his own cock, equally amazed and conflicted when he'd worked out how to make himself come.

It felt good enough for him, but that didn't mean it would be for anyone else.

Levi licked at his ear in panting little breaths. "Daddy? Pleeeeeease, Daddy…"

Fuck it. He didn't know how long he'd been hesitating, but all of his hypotheticals about "someone" seeing or touching him were moot. His boy was already whimpering in desire and thrusting against his leg at just the opportunity to hold his dick in his hand. He didn't sound tired any more, just horny and desperate.

It was a heady sensation, knowing that he could do this to his boy, exactly as he was.

Still clenching Levi's hand under his own, they explored his cock together. It felt like part of him. Like his boy was stroking him, feeling how hard he was for him. Making him feel good, just like he'd begged to do.

He guided Levi's hand faster, pulling the loose skin up and down. It already felt amazing, and if he could just get the angle and the pressure right… there. He heard himself moaning. There were ridges on the inside that rubbed against his base dick, and every time their linked hands slammed down it was like Levi was right there touching him.

"Oh, yes, Daddy," Levi whispered. "Can I taste you? Please, Abbale."

Saul hadn't planned on this. Maybe in a few

months. Maybe when he'd worked up the courage to lick the thing himself.

There wasn't really a point to it anyway. It would look hot as fuck, but it would probably taste plasticky and weird for Levi and Saul wouldn't be able to feel it. The only real benefit would be the idea of watching Levi take his cock, and for that, he figured he'd at least want to set up the right scene.

"It probably tastes gross," he heard himself saying. Not the best introduction. He should have just said no or stood up to his fears and let Levi at least have a look.

Levi giggled. "You know what tastes gross, Daddy? Cum. It's disgusting." He didn't need to see Levi's face to know he was wrinkling his nose. "I bet this will be much better."

While he tried to decide, Levi took over the rhythm. He'd figured out the trick of slamming down hard on each stroke, and Saul found himself arching up into each one. He let his fingers relax over Levi's, holding his underwear out of the way and just brushing the back of Levi's eager hand and the ridge of his own cock.

Saul found himself moaning. This was right. This was what it was supposed to feel like with his boy working his cock.

"Do you like that, Daddy? Do you feel good?"

Fuck. Couldn't he tell? Saul hadn't had anyone get him off in so long, and this right here, with Levi's dirty little moans and hand on his dick was ecstasy. He grunted out an affirmative.

Levi groaned again, breath hot and rapid across his neck. "Thank you, Daddy. Taste you… maybe later. Just want you to come."

Levi didn't sound disappointed with the plan. He sounded needy and desperate.

Levi had already shown Saul that so many of his doubts and insecurities were unfounded. His boy not only accepted him completely but couldn't get enough of him. His boy was hungry for this.

So if this was the treat Levi wanted… Saul realized that he wanted to give it to him. Maybe give it to both of them. "Turn around, boy."

Levi made an interrogative noise.

"Ass up here. Mouth on my cock."

"Oh, yes, Daddy! Thank you, Daddy."

Levi scrambled around as they figured out the cumbersome organization of getting Levi's knees past Saul's shoulders and a pillow under Saul's head. Their height difference didn't make anything any easier. Saul pulled his cock through the front panel of his briefs, wishing he'd thought to do it before Levi was staring at him.

But when Levi moaned as he took it into his mouth, all of the awkwardness washed away. Through the arch of Levi's slender body, Saul could see his jaw split open as he took it all inside. Oh, God. That was hotter than he'd imagined.

Levi's hand landed around the base, anchoring his cock and adding to the sensation. Sloppy and eager,

Levi set up a rhythm that had Saul already jerking up against him.

And then there was Levi's dick, hard and red and rubbing along his cheek. When he looked upward, all he could see was tight balls, firm cock, and the curve of Levi's ass.

Saul brought the head to his lips, exploring the spongy texture and tangy taste. Levi moaned and did *something* with his hands and mouth that ground right into Saul's base dick.

Saul didn't have the deep-throating confidence that Levi did, but he could still use his other hand, gorging himself on Levi's smooth skin and noisy enjoyment.

He set up a slow stroking rhythm, which Levi matched a moment later. God, his beautiful boy. Still telling him, in a million ways, that he wanted to follow his Daddy's lead.

Saul picked up the pace and Levi echoed it. They were a circle, complete like this. Daddy and boy. Cocks and mouths. And such glorious pleasure echoing between and through them.

Finally, Saul reached the pace that he wanted. He reached his other hand down to adjust things, keeping Levi's pressure right where he needed it. The rapid, steady beat was taking them both closer to the edge, and he found himself moaning around Levi's cock.

"Daddy?" Levi arched back. "Need to come. Can I come?"

Saul took the boy's throbbing dick out of his mouth

to answer. "This isn't a scene, baby. It's just us. Come when you want to."

"Thank you, Daddy. Want you to come, too."

Saul sucked him down again. There was no better response. He was so close. Needed this so much. Needed the perfection of his boy's noisy sucking and muffled moans while ecstasy raced through Saul's body at every thrust.

Saul sucked harder, giving up any attempt at finesse. His hand was a blur on Levi's shaft and Levi matched his pace.

Then everything came crashing through him. He thrust up and reared back, completely forgetting to work the cock in his hand.

It was all he could do to hang on as pleasure raced through him, like lightning and fire, burning him up.

He came against Levi's eager lips, bucking up to chase the sensation while Levi, sensing his need, ground down against him.

Everything came together, perfect and whole.

Then, with a muffled cry, Levi was spurting into his mouth, thrusting convulsively. Saul tongued around him, giving him a few loose strokes as Levi shook and screamed and clung to him.

When he finally drew in a deep ragged breath, Levi was still sucking on him, the soft echoes of pleasure bringing them down together.

"Come up here, baby."

The second he pronounced the words, Levi flipped around and settled onto his chest, squeezing him tightly with arms and legs. His dick was soft on Saul's belly, sweet and snuggly. Saul's own cock, of course, was still hard despite his utter lethargy. Maybe he could reach in to adjust it downward later.

Levi sought his mouth, and he pulled the boy into a sensuous kiss, their breath and lips tangling together.

As their pulses slowed, Levi rested his head on Saul's shoulder. They were both sweaty and sticky, but when Saul tried to roll them over, Levi just clung harder.

"I'll be right back, my motek. I just want to get us cleaned up."

"Not yet. Need more Daddy."

"You haven't had enough yet?"

Levi shook his sweaty curls against Saul's neck. "Never."

"What if I ran you a bath?" Saul figured he could take a quick shower and then fill the tub after he got dressed. He loved the idea of giving Levi a bath and scrubbing him clean.

"Nope. Nap time. And you hold me."

"Then let me go get a washcloth for you and a quick wash-up for me." The packer and harness were starting to irritate his skin as the sweat and other fluids dried.

"Fine," Levi huffed. "But you have to come right back."

"Promise." He gave Levi another kiss and finally managed to disentangle himself.

He came back first to wipe Levi down with a warm cloth, enjoying how Levi languidly stretched and uncurled himself to allow him access and then cuddled back up again.

"Now snuggle me," Levi demanded when he was done.

"I need to clean up too, sweet boy." He stroked Levi's hair and got a nose wrinkle in return. "Go to sleep and I'll be here soon."

"Hurry."

"I will." He gave him a little kiss. How anyone could complain about having a boyfriend who was so *greedy* that he demanded faster cuddles was beyond him.

He knew, even as he promised, that "soon" would still take a while. If he were a cis guy, he could have just wiped off his hand on the sheet or whatever other gross things most men seemed to do, but right now he was feeling kind of itchy and sticky. Definitely not at all tired.

In the bathroom, he cleaned Levi's buttplug and set it on a clean towel.

Then he stripped, stepped into the shower for a quick rinse, and put on a clean t-shirt from his overnight bag. He hand-washed his packer and harness, but he couldn't decide what to do with the harness.

Sex toys on towels, or really on kitchen counters, laundry bins, and dishwashers for that matter, were perfectly normal. This felt different, though. It was very personal in a way that he couldn't quite quantify.

But the stretchy fabric definitely needed to air dry. Reluctantly, he hung it over the shower pole. He didn't want it staying damp all night, and there really wasn't anywhere else to put it in Levi's small apartment.

The packer, at least, he could still wear like he normally did. He dried it off carefully with another towel and gave it a shake of the cornstarch-based powder to avoid chafing. Then he slipped on a pair of briefs and tucked it into the special pocket in front that separated it from his skin. With the inner rod removed, it hung limp and heavy against him, pleasantly filling out his underwear.

He considered himself for another minute to check himself over, especially his shirt without a binder. Levi hadn't commented earlier, maybe hadn't even noticed. There were still two visible bumps, especially when he turned to the side. Ugh.

On the other hand, Levi was sleeping. And he'd already proven, again and again, that he accepted Saul's body. Maybe it was alright for Saul to start accepting it more too.

He crept back into the room and wrapped himself around Levi's back. It was probably silly, since his head only came up to Levi's shoulders at this angle. But he liked it. It made him feel strong and protective.

"Daddy," Levi murmured happily. Then he ground back with his ass against Levi's soft cock.

"Go to sleep, naughty boy."

Levi hummed sleepily. "Just want you close."

It wouldn't do any good to point out that they were already pressed together from head to toe. Levi would always want more, and he adored that. "I'm here," he said instead.

He still wasn't tired, but he could relax a bit while they snuggled.

"Christy was right," Levi commented, though he still sounded only half awake.

"Hmmm?" Saul kept his voice quiet in case Levi wasn't talking to him, but just drifting into sleep.

"Yeah. This was just like a Hallmark movie and a Hanukkah miracle, but with more porn."

Saul's laugh shook them both. "Yeah, baby?"

"Mmmm-hmmm… perfect."

Saul cuddled his boy while he slept. His neshama. His soul.

And it was, in fact, perfect.

A LITTLE BONUS FOR YOU

OK, so I couldn't help it. I just wanted Christy to get with Nikhil so badly… and they did! *Office Appropriate* is a femdom hurt/comfort short story with humiliation kink and a HEA. You can download it from Prolific-Works for free!

And if you loved this book, there are **nine more sweet and bratty boys** out there in the Naughty or Nice series to take home for your very own!

You can read more about *ArmyBratBoy* and *English-DaddyInNY* in Colette Davison's book Dear Daddy, Please Hold Us. (Hehehe. I have so much fun writing them into this book!) And the next book coming out is Dear Daddy, Please Praise Me by two of my favorite authors, Amy Bellows and Luna David.

※

If you enjoyed this book, please leave a review! Amazon and GoodReads reviews mean a lot to authors for sharing their work with even more readers. Even taking a couple of minutes to rank the book and write a few words makes a big difference. ;)

You can hang out with me on Facebook in **Reese Morrison's Rebels** where there are teasers released (almost) every week. Or sign up for my newsletter for updates about releases along with teasers and book recommendations.

ABOUT THE AUTHOR

Reese Morrison lives in Philadelphia with their partner, two precocious children, and intermittent housemates, guests, and homeless, queer teens. Their hobbies are volunteering on too many boards, planting gardens that they forget to water halfway through the summer, making up songs for their kids, and putting off writing their dissertation.

Reese and their partner both identify as genderqueer and are part of a vibrant community of queer and trans folks. They started writing because they were dissatisfied with the lack of trans and genderqueer characters in what they were reading and finally decided to do something about it. Many, but not all, of their books are kinky (for a whole range of kinks...) and they feel that it's important to represent a range of backgrounds, dis/abilities, gender presentations/ identities, and body types in their writing.

Is Reese Jewish? Yes! How did you guess?

His for Hanukkah

Most people like vacations. And Christmas. But Adam is Jewish and spending the season alone, wishing he had a Daddy.

Returning back to town after several years and now living as a transgender man, Tate worries when hitting on his friend Adam seems to scare him away. But when Tate finds out that Adam's anxiety disorder was making it difficult to connect, they agree to spend Hanukkah together.

Now Tate has eight nights to seduce, pamper, and claim his boy. But will it be enough for Tate to keep him after the holiday's over?

His for Hanukkah contains a Daddy/boy dynamic, chastity, spankings, cuddles, the sexiest latkes ever, and a HEA.

Find *His for Hanukkah* on Amazon and Kindle Unlimited.

Love Language

A younger Dom. A grieving sub. Two men whose kinks don't match (or so they think) connecting in ASL.

Marco and Greg would both rather be anywhere than a kink club on Valentine's Day. Marco doesn't have the patience to speech-read in a hearing crowd. And Greg is still mourning his Sir who passed away three years ago.

But when Greg steps in to explain something in ASL, Marco can't stop thinking about the light he sees in those sad eyes. Strong, older, fluent in sign language, and sweetly submissive, Greg is exactly Marco's type. Even if Greg isn't ready for another relationship yet, Marco isn't ready to let him go.

Greg thought that he would never want to date someone again. But as painful as it is to admit, he's starting to feel like it might be time. Marco is like no one he's never met. Small, twink-ish, over a decade younger, and a Daddy, he isn't at all what Greg imagined in a Dom. Yet he's undeniably attracted to his care and control, even after Marco reveals that he's transgender. Slipping into ASL, the language of his childhood, Greg wonders if he might have a second chance at love.

This book contains hurt/comfort themes, predicament bondage, Shibari, wax, and CNC role play, just to get started... and a HEA ending.

Find *Love Language* on Amazon and Kindle Unlimited.

Love Lessons

"Come here," Dustin repeated, his dark eyes serious.

Landon put his hands on his hips and stood his ground. "Make me."

He knew he was acting like a petulant teenager, but this was Dustin. And with Dustin, he felt safe.

Please, *he thought,* please, please make me.

Landon doesn't need anyone. So he's confident that when he offers to train a nervous, sexy Dom, nothing will come of it.

But Dustin has some things to teach him, too. Because

Dustin uses sign language and asks him questions that no one else bothers to ask. Because Dustin wants him, no matter how he presents his gender. Because when Landon rebels, Dustin's there to keep him in line. And when Dustin makes him obey, it feels real.

Real enough to call Dustin his Daddy.

But these are just lessons, right?

Love Lessons has a nervous new Dom, a confident and genderfluid sub who offers to train him, age play with a middle, a bit of angst, and plenty of sign language. This book is the second in the Love Language series, but it can be read alone.

Find *Love Lessons* on Amazon and Kindle Unlimited.

Love Limits

Ash wants a Daddy. Zhong wants Ash.

But Zhong knows he can't give Ash what they need. He's asexual, and when he looks for someone special, it should be someone who will be satisfied with what he can offer. Right?

As Zhong grows closer to the flirty sub, he learns more about himself. Maybe he can be the Daddy that Ash needs. And maybe he can have the family that he never expected to have.

Maybe his love doesn't have to have limits.

Love Limits contains a caring asexual Daddy, a flirty genderqueer sub, polyamory, puppy play, and a HEA for everyone. This is the third book in the Love Language series, and it should be read as a companion to *Love Lessons*.

Love Limits will be available in Spring 2021.

Hummingbird Tales

Hummingbird and Kraken

Geir

Geir lives alone in the woods for a reason. And he likes it that way.

Until Declan lands on his doorstep, with a bubbly personality, shimmery lipstick, and dreams of adventure. Surely he can let him stay for a few days without giving in to temptation.

Or letting him discover that he's a kraken shifter.

Only Declan has other ideas. Because Declan loves his tentacles. And he believes that Geir can be the Daddy that he needs.

Declan

Declan might be a teeny, little bit impulsive. Alright, a lot impulsive. But he's still allowed to believe in love at first sight, right? Geir is practically perfect, with his stern scowl, sexy secret, and possessive doting. When Declan settles in and makes friends with the neighboring shifter tribe, it feels like he might have found a home.

Of course, it isn't that easy.

Strangers lurk in the area, harassing Declan for information about his shifter friends. Geir inexplicably disappears for hours every day. Declan's only clues seem to lie in Native American legends, as he tries to unravel Geir's past and their future together.

When danger threatens their small community, Declan's

loyalty is put to the test. And Geir must decide who he trusts, who he cares about, and who he is.

"Hummingbird and Kraken" is an expansion of the short story "My Kraken." It has non-mpreg shifters, a happy-go-lucky boy, a grumpy old kraken, bad guys on the loose, plenty of tentacles, and a HEA.

Find *The Hummingbird's Gift* on Amazon and Kindle Unlimited.

The Hummingbird's Gift

What if the gods got it wrong?

When children in Rohahen's tribe come of age, they receive shifter forms from the gods. Sometimes these forms come with an extra gift: strength-sharers can give mental commands while heart-singers can shape others' emotions.

Rohahen has been hiding his crush on Tier for fifteen years. For the balance of the tribe, the Chief must marry a heart-singer, not a strength-sharer like himself.

Only Rohahen is starting to wonder if there might be other ways of being a heart-singer. When Tier starts to return his affection, perhaps he can find the bravery to show the world who he really is.

Because the ways of the gods are mysterious. And maybe they didn't get it wrong after all.

The Hummingbird's Gift is a companion to *Hummingbird and Kraken* and continues the story of one if its primary characters. (It will not make sense as a stand-alone.) It is a friends-to-lovers story with an adorable bison shifter, an uncertain Chief, a heart-singer coming into his own, plenty of heat, and a HEA.

Find *The Hummingbird's Gift* on Amazon and Kindle Unlimited.

Whirlwind

A magical moment.

A single night.

A collection of stories about first kisses, second chances, kinky explorations, and having the confidence to ask for what you want.

Five whirlwind relationships celebrating queer bodies and queer love.

Waiting for You: Taylor has been pining for his best friend, Julio, for most of his life. But he knows that he's too big, too fat, and too plain to ever appeal. It doesn't help that his secret desires for lace, makeup, and submission don't match his outsides at all. He could never catch Julio's eye, could he? (MM, friends-to-lovers)

Here for You: Eric has always avoided dating. But something's different about the new sub, Micah. He's both vulnerable and strong, owning his disability, his transgender identity, and his unconventional desires. Eric is happy to arrange a group scene for the night... and perhaps look for something more tomorrow. (MM, first time)

Game for You: Ben and Parker have been circling each other for years in a frenzy of insane dares and sexual innuendo. But as two Doms, they know they could never get together. Enter sassy, gorgeous Dakota, a perfect mix of masculine and feminine, and a perfect challenge for the two men to claim. This story contains spanking, whipping, an erotic game of darts, and an even sexier bet. (MMX, friends-to-lovers with someone new)

Back for You: When Nina was betrayed by her teenaged crush at their all-male boarding school, she vowed to move on in her life. She transitioned to being the woman she always knew she was and didn't look back. But when she meets a gorgeous new customer, it takes only a moment to recognize those eyes. Angel has a new name, but she's as intense and commanding as ever. And she wants to ask for another chance. This story contains role play, spankings, foot worship, and a chance to reclaim the one who got away. (FF, second chance)

Time for You: Charlie knows that she's too old and grumpy for someone like Carla. He's young, dapper, confident, and most of all, just as butch as she is. It's easier to just ignore his flirting and push away any hope for something between them. What would that even look like? When Carla asks her out, Charlie has to decide. Can she take the risk to not only trust Carla, but explore sides of herself she never dared to face? And if she does, will Carla still want her? This story contains shibari and first-time submission. (XX, friends-to-lovers, younger Dom/older sub)

The first three stories (Waiting for You, Here for You, and Game for You) were previously released as separate volumes.

Find *Whirlwind* on Amazon and Kindle Unlimited.

Music to My Ears

In a world is full of music celebrating straight relationships, the Music to My Ears series imagines stories behind popular songs when a pronoun change gives them a whole new meaning. These books are connected by a theme, rather than characters, and they may be read in any order.

Jesse's Girl

When Julia meets her perfect boyfriend over a couple of guitar riffs at her summer job, she holds herself back from lighting up every time he plays her signature song and makes her smile. Because no matter how she feels inside, Jesse will only ever see her as an awkward, gangly boy named Jude. Being best friends and bandmates will have to be enough, because she knows it's all she'll ever get.

Jesse just can't figure it out. Jude is his best friend. His perfect match. He might not be attracted to him, but he can't imagine a future without Jude in it. So when Jude takes off after graduation within a word, he's devastated.

Their friendship has always come easily, but it might not withstand Julia's homophobic father or Jesse discovering the truth. There's no way Julia could ever become... Jesse's girl.

Find *Jesse's Girl* on Amazon and Kindle Unlimited.

THANK YOU

Endless gratitude to the beta readers and proofreaders who caught developmental gaps, typos, and continuity errors, as well as advising me on their experiences with various identities and bodies Abrianna, Jo, Kat, Michelle, Misty, Renee, Sabella, Tara, you guys rock!

Thank you to Cate Ashwood for the gorgeous cover.

Thank you to Chara Croft for the fantastic feedback and making me write one more dirty chapter.

Many thanks to Rheland Richmond for formatting this series.

As always, thank you to my partner for supporting me while I'm glued to the computer for many more hours than I say I will be, pretty much every day. ;)

PSST... ONE MORE TIME

If you're looking for Christy and Nikhil's story, *Office Appropriate,* you can download it from ProlificWorks for free!